On the Run
with a Supervillain

Supervillain Romance Project

H. L. Burke

For information about H. L. Burke's latest novels, to sign up
for the author's newsletter, or to contact the author, go to
www.hlburkeauthor.com

Free eBook for Newsletter Subscribers!

To Isabell[a]
Save th[...]

D1714171

To Brownie Bite, the little cat with a big attitude.
—Heidi

Chapter One

Cloaked in darkness, Shawn Park, AKA Surge, crouched on the roof of the building across from the two story brick structure that housed Great River Legacy Bank. Streetlights illuminated an empty parking lot, and faint light shone from within. Something moved behind a second floor window. Shawn tapped his earpiece.

"I see someone on the second floor, third window in. Anyone else?"

"I've tapped into the security cameras. It's just the night watchman, Park," Crystal, the team captain, a veteran superhero with invisibility powers, replied over the comm. "I know you're eager to get your first real takedown on the books, but trust me, newbie, there's a lot of waiting in superheroing."

Shawn bit his tongue. This would *not* be his first takedown. A little over a year before he'd gone up against a vengeful villain named Mythcreant who had chosen bringing Shawn down as his life's goal. Shawn had prevailed in that challenge, but since it was not an official Department of Super-Abled mission, most DOSA sables, short for super-ableds, didn't count it towards his record.

He would've liked for his team to stop treating him like a complete greenhorn, but as the newest and, at twenty-three, the youngest member, he had the common sense to keep his pride in line and just accept the ribbing.

"I'm with the new guy," Rapidz, the team's speed sable, moaned. Shawn glanced towards the far corner of the roof where he knew her to be stationed. Rapidz, whose non-handle name was Rita Diaz, stirred in the shadows. "Are we sure of our intel? We've been waiting for hours."

"My source is reliable," Maestro chimed in. "He didn't even know I had ears in the room so he had no reason to lie."

Even though Maestro was stationed on the other side of the bank from Shawn, the younger man's skin still crawled. Maestro called his powers "puppeting" but what that essentially meant was he could put himself in a trance-like state and project himself into other people's bodies for short periods, seeing through their eyes, hearing through their ears, and even taking over their actions. So far Shawn had only seen him doing this on training missions, but Crystal would sometimes send Maestro to project himself into haunts frequented by those connected to the villain scene and have him listen in for tips.

That was how the team had learned that a safety deposit box in this particular bank held something of enough value to have attracted Abounder, a villain with size-manipulation powers who specialized in high-end robberies.

The target was a diamond, recently transferred from a private home with top-of-the-line security due to the owner's sudden death. Apparently the valuable gem had caused a squabble among heirs, and the executor had taken it into protective custody until the matter could be settled.

Abounder had gotten the tip from a disgruntled employee, and Maestro had been certain that the heist would be going down that night.

"Honestly, I'm fine if the guy doesn't show up."

Shawn started. This time the voice wasn't in his ear but came from behind him. He spun, his powers kicking in and pushing him a foot off the ground.

Rick, the team's fifth member, jumped back a step. "Easy!" he held up his hands. Ice crystals shimmered about his fingers as if he'd sprinkled his extremities in glitter. Rick's hero handle was Pleistocene—which Shawn still wasn't confident in pronouncing so he was glad the guy was cool about being called by his given name. From what he could tell, Rick was never un-cool about anything.

Appropriate considering his powers.

"Aren't you supposed to be down there?" Shawn pointed towards the alley behind the bank.

"Crystal took over there and told me to come up here," Rick said.

Shawn's stomach twisted. There was only one reason Crystal would've told Rick to change posts: she wanted someone to babysit the new guy.

Man, I need a chance to prove myself. He dropped his powers, and his feet hit the roof again.

Rick leaned against the wall that surrounded the edge of the roof. He was small framed, a few inches shorter than average-sized Shawn, late-thirties with a goatee and brown hair pulled back in a ponytail. Unlike Shawn, who wore a full uniform of blue body armor, he chose to work in a pair of cargo shorts and a worn flannel shirt, seemingly oblivious to the cold night air.

"You think Maestro's intel might be off?" Shawn

asked after making sure his comm wasn't transmitting.

Rick shrugged. "I doubt we'll be that lucky. I've worked with the guy for over a decade, and he's been wrong maybe twice in that time ... and one of those times the villain *had* planned something, but he'd gotten sidelined by his own premature celebration. We eventually found him passed out, missing his pants, and surrounded by empty bottles a block from the target he'd planned to hit."

"Sounds like an easy take-down," Shawn said.

"The guy threw up all over the backseat when we were taking him in." Rick made a gagging sound. "Personally, I would've preferred fighting him to cleaning up after that. The guy had gone out for sushi the night before too. I haven't really had the stomach for seafood since that day."

"Sorry," Shawn said.

"Hazards of the job. Once you've been in the game as long as the rest of us have, you'll realize that superheroing is primarily an occasional half hour of excitement followed by a lot of paperwork and months of waiting around." Rick rolled his shoulders. "Speaking of time off, you're leaving tomorrow?"

In spite of his nerves, Shawn's chest lightened. "Yeah. Going to spend the holidays with my family and my girlfriend."

He hadn't seen Katie since he'd joined the team. Between her on-going training as part of the Supervillain Rehabilitation Project and his own DOSA related duties, they could at best squeeze in a few video calls a week these days. Man, he wanted to see her again. Badly.

"Nice. Glad to meet someone who still has a life outside of DOSA." Rick snorted.

Shawn managed not to laugh. With his girlfriend in the SVR and his father the team leader for DOSA's Columbus branch, Shawn's life was hopelessly entangled with DOSA. Of course, he didn't mind that so much.

"Got something!" Rapidz's eager voice went off in Shawn's ears, and he gripped the wall to keep himself from flying into the air again. "Crystal, do we have any eyes on the eastern corner of the building? I see something there."

"There's a camera covering the rear entrance ... yeah you're right. Something's moving ... crap, it's him. He's about the size of a house cat and getting smaller. He just slipped under the door. Dang it. He's already in."

Shawn's muscles tensed.

"Go in, team. Now! Park, Rick, from the front. We know he's after the deposit box, so head there. Rapidz, help me cover the exits so he doesn't double back and escape. Maestro, you're surveillance. Everyone got their disruptors?"

Shawn tapped his pocket. "Yes, Ma'am." His voice echoed three other affirmative responses. He glanced at Rick. "Need a lift?"

"Got it covered." Rick flicked his wrist towards the parking lot below and a ramp of ice formed, creating a natural slide. He swung over the wall and whooshed down, landing seconds later on the concrete.

That looks fun.

Shawn debated using the same form of exit, but not wanting to embarrass himself, he leaped up then swooped down. The cool night air rushed through his dark hair as he skidded to a halt next to Rick.

A blur of silver-blue darted down the alley at the back of the bank: Rapidz going at full tilt. Shawn assumed Crystal was somewhere near there as well, but with her powers, it was impossible to be certain. Maestro, of course, would be working remotely. No need for him to get his hands dirty.

"Can you get into his head, Maestro?" Crystal asked over the comm.

"Nah, his powers are up. Always short circuits mine," Maestro replied. "I can hop into the security guard if you want my eyes in the building."

"No, keep him out of it. Watch him, though. If he starts to wander into danger, grab him and turn him around."

Shawn alighted to one side of the glass doors as Rick skated to a halt on the other. Squinting through the glass, Shawn couldn't make out anything but an empty bank lobby. The action, though, would be in the vault, where the safety deposit boxes were.

"Going in the back now," Crystal said. "Cover the front, boys. We'll try to flush him out your way."

"Roger." Rick opened a panel to the side of the door and keyed in a code. The doors swooshed open. "We're entering the lobby. Will wait for instructions."

In spite of Shawn's previous confidence, his pulse pounded painfully as he stepped onto the tiles of the bank's lobby. His eyes flicked over the area: teller counter, mortgage offices, a lot of awful looking fake plants. Pretty standard bank stuff.

Come on. Get it together.

He swallowed to moisten his dry tongue.

Five heroes against one villain. The odds are stacked in our favor. I need to simply not screw up.

"At the vault. No sign of the mark."

Shawn exchanged a glance with Rick at Crystal's announcement.

"He can get pretty small. Do you think he slipped into the vault?" Rick asked.

"If he did, he's stuck in there if he wants to take any loot with him. He can't shrink down objects, only himself, according to his DOSA profile," Shawn put in, proud of himself that he'd read the entire packet on this guy. "Whatever he wants in that vault, it's staying there."

"Wouldn't be the first time a DOSA file missed a super ability," Rapidz pointed out.

"I can sense him," Maestro broke in. "He's making his way out through the front. Headed towards the lobby."

6

"I got this." Rick stepped towards the entrance to the back, an enforced door with an "employees only" label, hands extended. His fingers shimmered before sheets of ice burst from his palms. With a sound like breaking glass, it hit the door. A layer of sparkling ice formed over the entrance, sealing all the cracks.

Shawn gave a low whistle. "Nice work."

"Try to slip through that, Microman," Rick said.

Shawn glanced at him. "You into retro-gaming?"

"I'm into classics." Rick smiled. "Now if you want to talk true golden oldies—"

The building shook. Shawn's powers jolted to life, sending a blast of energy in front of him like a shield.

The door exploded, raining shards of ice down on both men. Ice pattered harmlessly against Shawn's shield which he extended to cover Rick.

"Rick, Surge! Report in!" Crystal barked.

Shawn gaped. A fist the size of a microwave retracted towards where a man proportional to it was crammed into the narrow hallway like a fat cat squeezing into a box. Sheetrock dust rained from the strained ceiling.

"Crap," Rick muttered.

"He's here!" Shawn yelped into his comm, his words coming out way squeakier than he would've preferred.

Abounder's body vibrated before shrinking down to the size of a normal human being. He darted forward. Shawn drew all his powers into his fist and swung. His energy created a boxing glove like field around his hand and arm. It collided against Abounder, knocking the man backwards into the customer service desk. The pressboard structure gave out with a resounding crash.

"Freeze!" Rick snarled. He whipped a line of ice across the villain's chest, pinning him against the floor.

Abounder grunted and writhed, straining against the ice. The frozen restraints creaked and cracked as Abounder began to vibrate again.

"Crystal, Rapidz, hurry!" Shawn barked out. "We can't

hold him for long."

"Disruptor cuffs!" The irritation in Crystal's tone bit at Shawn's pride.

Well, duh. He pulled a coiled disruptor cuff from his utility belt and darted forward. A blast of ice hit him in the back. He stumbled.

"Sorry!" Rick said. "I didn't realize you were stepping there—"

Shawn picked himself up. Too late.

Abounder exploded from the ice, swelling to fill half the lobby. His expanding knee hit Shawn, knocking him back into a wall. Rick gave a muffled cry.

"We can't get through. The hallway's collapsed." Rapidz cursed. "Gonna try to come around the front."

"What if he doubles back?" Maestro broke in.

Shawn tried to rise, but a massive foot pinned him to the wall. He gasped for breath. Where was the disruptor cuff? Could he even get it around Abounder at his current size? With all that remained of his strength, he threw his power into one more blast.

The shock wave slammed into the gigantic supervillain. With a shout, Abounder flew backwards, through the window in a rain of glass. Shawn staggered to his feet just in time to see Abounder pick himself up, vibrate, and shrink down too small to be seen.

A streak of silvery blue skidded to a halt a few feet away a second later. A groan from the demolished teller counter drew Shawn's attention to Rick, lying amongst the wreckage. Hurrying over, Shawn offered him a hand up.

"You all right?" he asked.

"Winded. Pride sprained." Rick winced.

"I can't find him!" Rapidz stomped her feet in the parking lot as if hoping she might squash Abounder by sheer chance. "Maestro?"

"On my way down, but I can't get a track on him. Sorry."

Crystal popped into visibility in the center of the lobby. Her gaze swept over the chaos of the half-demolished bank, and she grimaced. "Great. Headquarters is going to love this."

As if in answer, sirens blared in the distance.

Shawn stiffened. "Should we tell the police to stay back? What if Abounder regroups and tries again."

"I doubt he will. I've already got a DOSA clean up crew enroute." Crystal's shoulders slumped. "At least we foiled the robbery, though we probably cost the bank as much in property damage." Her eyes zeroed in on Shawn and Rick. "What happened? Why didn't one of you get a disruptor cuff on him?"

Rick's gaze dropped to his feet. "I thought I could hold him with my powers. It was a misjudgment. Sorry, Crys."

Shawn stayed quiet. He'd been about to snap on a cuff when Rick had hit him ... but he didn't want to go on record throwing one of his teammates under the bus on his first real mission. "I should've been faster. I'm sorry, too."

"Obviously, we all need some training here." Crystal continued to scowl. "Powers are all well and good, but getting a disruptor on the target should always be the first priority. Rapidz, get upstairs and check on the security guard. He's probably the one who called in the normie police. Pleistocene, go to the vault and make sure it's secure. I doubt Abounder will try again tonight, but if he does, I want you there."

"Yes, ma'am." Rick nodded and started down the hallway.

Rapidz gave their team leader a thumbs up and headed for the stairs.

Shawn shifted from foot to foot, hyper aware that he hadn't been given an assignment. He'd done his best, and it wasn't as if the whole responsibility for the failure rested on him—but dang, he'd wanted his first mission to go better.

The black SUVs of the DOSA clean up crew arrived seconds after the police cruisers. Rapidz returned with the security guard, her face drawn.

"Hey, Crystal, we've got a problem," she said.

"What now?" Crystal asked.

"I'll let him explain." Rapidz motioned towards the security guard.

The man stepped forward and let out a breath. "The first step after an incident, according to policy, is for the guard on duty—me, in this case—to pull the security tapes and make copies for the authorities ... I started to do this, but—they've been wiped."

Crystal's jaw fell. "How? We were here the whole time Abounder was here. He didn't have an opportunity to do that."

"I'm not sure. I didn't see anyone enter the control center, and it should be impervious to outside attacks." The guard's voice sank to a mumble. "At least that's what the brochure says."

The color drained from Crystal's face. "I need to check on something."

She jogged down the hall. A sinking feeling in his gut, Shawn followed.

They stopped before the vault door where Rick now leaned, fiddling with his phone.

"Hey, Crys." He gave Crystal an easy smile.

"I need to check inside." She motioned towards the door.

His brow furrowed. "Why? We're pretty sure we spooked the target before he got a chance to get in there, right?"

"I need to be sure."

Rick peeled himself off the wall. Crystal hurried to the control panel, punching in a security code. The door seal gave with a hiss, and she opened it.

Shawn's heart dropped into his stomach. A wall of

tiny doors faced him, all conspicuously closed—except one. That door hung open, the space beyond it cavernously empty.

"How?" Rick breathed.

Chapter Two

Shawn's vision blurred as he stared at the screen before him.

"So much paperwork."

Rick snickered from his seat at the other team computer across the shared office space. Shawn had his own desktop for gaming and personal use in his room, but he liked doing the monotonous stuff around other people. Apparently so did Rick, who now gave him a commiserating look. "Told you that was 90% of what we do."

Shawn glanced at the time on his screen. Nearly 7:30 a.m. He'd been up all night, but as much as he wanted to quit, he needed to get his reports filed before he left. He was driving to Columbus, so he didn't have the tight time clock of making a flight, but if he wanted to get there before tomorrow when Katie was flying in from Wichita, he'd have to leave today. If he could get done in the next half hour, he *might* have time for a catnap before he had to leave.

Rapidz, whose speed powers apparently also applied to typing out reports, had already disappeared, as had Maestro. Crystal had shut herself in her private office to stew over the defeat. Shawn didn't blame her. He'd gone over everything he'd done during the course of the mission countless times, trying to find out where he'd screwed up and what he could've done to prevent the disaster.

Rick stood. "Done, thank God. I'm going to turn in. I'm guessing you'll be gone by the time I emerge from hibernation, so I'll see you again after the holidays."

"I'll see you too. Maybe we can talk classic games together." Shawn shot him a weary smile.

"Yeah, sounds like a plan."

After Rick left, Shawn refocused on his report. He should've asked Rick how to handle getting hit by one of Rick's ice bolts. Sure, he hadn't been hurt by it, but the slight delay it had caused might've prevented Shawn from getting the disruptor cuff on Abounder—or maybe Shawn would've failed at that even without the distraction.

Nah, it's not a big enough deal to risk making a teammate look bad. It might even seem like I'm trying to blame him for the failure to take the onus off myself. Not a great look for my first mission with the team.

He saved his report and forwarded it to Crystal's email address.

Standing, he stretched. Man. He needed this vacation.

"Hey, Park."

Crystal's voice spun him to face the doorway.

His team leader's gaze took in the room. "I need to talk to you alone for a minute."

His stomach twisted. "I'm sorry I wasn't quicker tonight."

"You're not the only one at fault. Still, that was your first mission, and it sure coulda gone better." Her gray eyes drilled into him, and his chin dipped towards his chest. "Your dad's a good sable, I'd go as far as to say a great one," she continued.

He brightened. "Yeah, my dad's amazing. I've always —"

"Don't think because you're Dave Park's son you'll get to slide into this career," she interrupted. "If anything, I'm going to be harder on you than I would be to some random sable without the history. You've got a legacy to live up to. That's a responsibility, not a privilege."

His throat tightened. "Yes, ma'am."

She gave a slow nod. "I have a meeting with the bank officials and the DOSA clean up team this afternoon. Is your report turned in?"

"Just emailed it to you," he replied.

"Good. Get some rest and enjoy your time off." She walked away, leaving Shawn feeling like he'd been kicked in the gut.

He slouched towards the section of HQ devoted to personal quarters.

I can't fail at this. It's all I am. All I've ever wanted to be. If I can't hack it, then what am I even going to do with myself? How could I ever look Dad in the eye again?

He reached his door and entered. After quickly sloughing off his body armor, revealing his thin t-shirt and boxers beneath, he stretched out on his bed. Did he have time to sleep now? Did he even have a choice? He couldn't risk driving without some rest. Putting his phone on the charger, he tucked himself beneath his blankets and tried to get into a headspace where he could actually sleep.

His phone buzzed with an incoming video call from Katie.

His weariness lessened slightly, and he quickly answered. The camera clicked on, revealing her sitting in front of a wall covered in art prints, some of which he recognized as her personal, cartoon-inspired drawings. She smiled at him, her blue eyes shining. The tension in his chest eased.

"Sorry to call you so early, but I wanted to talk to you before you started driving." She tilted her head as if trying to look around him. "Are you in bed? I didn't wake you, did I?"

"No, I was already up."

Or he'd never had a chance to sleep, but he didn't need to burden her with that.

"Oh, good. I know you texted that you had a mission last night. Did it go okay?"

His lips pursed. "Not really. Target got away. I'm not even sure how—it's a long story."

"That sucks." She toyed with a strand of her fine red

hair. Man, what he wouldn't do to touch her hair right now … or any part of her for that matter. "That happens sometimes, though. Can't catch them all."

"I know, but it was my first mission with the team, and I feel responsible for it." He rubbed at his forehead.

Her lips twitched as if trying to hold back a smile. "Did you trip on your cape or something?"

"Not so much," he said. "It's not one thing I did in particular that was wrong so much as I just feel I could've done better overall at everything."

Sympathy flooded her beautiful eyes, and his world softened.

"Rain always tells me that everyone could always do better." Rain was Katie's mentor with the SVR, or Supervillain Rehabilitation project. Shawn had only met the woman briefly, but it seemed like Katie brought her up pretty much every time they talked. "You can't keep kicking yourself for past performances. You can only aim to be better in your next attempt, and considering this *was* your first mission, you definitely can only go up, right?"

"I guess." He mulled over his attitude. Maybe he was making a big deal out of this. Even Crystal had said the mission failure wasn't completely his fault. Still, what she'd said about his dad had hit him like Abounder's massive fist. "I kinda feel like everyone is expecting me to be good at this because I'm Verve's son. My dad is a lot to live up to, and … I'm not sure I've got it in me. What if I'm not hero material?"

"Don't be ridiculous." She frowned at him. "Of course you're hero material. You've already saved my life at least once. Also Ears, remember?"

He laughed. Ears was his basset hound, who he had adopted from a shelter after rescuing *all* the animals at that shelter from a fire. While he would've liked to bring Ears with him, he'd left him at his parents' for the last several months, not wanting to introduce the dog to his current posting until he was certain it was going to stick. He was looking forward to seeing Ears again over Christmas—not as much as he was looking forward to seeing Katie, but still, it was a bonus.

"You're not just a hero, Shawn. You're a superhero. A *super* superhero!" Her eyes twinkled. "And I should know. I've fought enough of them."

"I guess you have a unique perspective on heroes, then." He chuckled. "Come to think of it, if this hero thing doesn't work out, I might be calling you for some pointers on how to get in on the villain side of things."

Her nose scrunched. "Shawn, don't take this the wrong way, but you would be a horrible villain. You just don't have it in you."

A guffaw escaped him. "Yeah, you're right. I'll stick with the hero side." He glanced at the time. "I have a little packing left to do, and I've got to leave soon. Sorry to cut this short, but I really need to get started on all that."

"No worries. I just couldn't let you leave without getting to tell you I love you and please drive safely." She leaned closer to the phone until her face filled the whole screen. "I can't wait to hug you again, Shawn, and kiss you and ... oh, man, tomorrow can't come soon enough."

"Yeah, you're right." Something within him cracked open. With everything that had gone wrong, being with Katie felt like the one thing that could make everything right ... video calls were all well and good, but he wanted her present with him so much.

Why can't we always be together? Why can't I figure out how to make that a reality?

"I'll talk to you soon, okay? I love you." He hovered his finger over the "end call" button, unwilling to push it. She likewise stared at him, not hanging up on her end. She was the best thing in his life. Hanging up would be cutting his one connection to her, and even in the short term, he hated doing that.

Gritting his teeth, he hit the button, replaced the

phone on the charger, and settled into his bed.

This job has to work out, but more than that, Katie and I need to work out. DOSA is my career, but she's my life, my happiness.

A thought wormed its way into his heart and wouldn't let go.

It's time. I'm going to ask her to marry me. That way no matter what happens with DOSA, I at least have that.

Chapter Three

Waking up in his childhood room again, Shawn felt as if he'd traveled through time. The plastic glow-in-the-dark stars still twinkled on the ceiling, and the same space themed wallpaper that had been there since he was six—and bore the scars of many days of rough housing with his friends and sisters—still graced the walls. Something cold and wet nudged at his hand, and he rolled over in his twin bed to face Ears.

The basset hound rested his nose on the edge of the mattress, his tail thudding dully against the carpet.

"Hey, there, boy. Good to see you again." Shawn patted his dog's head.

Ears made a concerted effort to jump up next to Shawn but only managed to get his front legs onto the bed. He struggled to pull himself up the rest of the way. Shawn tugged him into a hug.

"Yeah, I missed you, too." He rubbed the dog's ears. Maybe once he'd settled into his team he could ask Crystal about having a dog in HQ. New recruits were required to live on site, and the single ones often chose to stay there for the cheap housing even after their probationary period was over. Shawn's team consisted completely of single people ... except for Shawn.

Of course I'm the one who has to rock the boat and challenge the team dynamic.

He shook his head wryly before gathering up a change of clothes and his toiletry bag and peeking out the door into the hall.

He'd gotten in late the night before. His parents had waited up, just to make sure he arrived safely, but he hadn't seen his sisters yet, even though he knew from the cars in the driveway they were both there. Now he could hear voices from down the hall. He'd go check in on them after he'd gotten a shower.

He'd just finished his shower and was meticulously applying toothpaste to his brush when someone slammed their fists against the bathroom door. He jumped, squirting toothpaste onto the bathroom counter.

"You've been in there for an hour," the familiar voice of Juliet, Shawn's youngest sister, whined. "I want my turn!"

"I've been in here for like ten minutes. You can wait." Shawn picked up a washcloth and wiped up the toothpaste.

"It's not fair, you barging in and taking over the bathroom," Juliet continued, her pout audible. "You don't live here anymore. I do!"

"Well, then, be a good hostess and go make sure my coffee is ready." He smirked at the door.

She huffed. Footsteps stomped away, heading down the hall.

Shawn laughed quietly. It was good to be the big brother.

He took his time with his grooming. His phone buzzed on the counter, and he picked it up.

New text from Katie.

His heart fluttered, and he tapped the notification.

Boarding now. See you in a few hours. I love you.

Butterflies swarmed his chest. He couldn't wait to see her again. He still wanted to talk to his dad about his determination to ask Katie to marry him. Not that he thought the discussion would change his mind, but somehow it felt wrong to go into this without at least asking his father what he thought.

He tapped out, **Can't wait to see you. Safe flight. I love you too.**

After sending it, he tucked his phone into his back pocket and opened the bathroom door.

He recoiled.

Juliet stood in the hallway, holding out a steaming mug of coffee, her expression sickeningly sweet. Her dark hair was done up in tight french braids, and she wore a pair of pink Hello Kitty pajamas, making her look even younger than her eighteen years.

He studied her suspiciously. "What did you do to it?"

"Mom said I should be nice to you because we don't get to see you very often." She held the cup a little higher. "She said I should be a peacemaker instead of a troublemaker."

"Huh." Shawn took the coffee and gave it a sniff. Seemed normal. He sneaked a fingertip into the liquid. Temperature was good. "Thanks," he said cautiously.

"You're welcome." She took a step back.

He hazarded a sip, and his eyes bulged. It was all he could do not to spit out the briny liquid onto his mom's beige carpet.

"Of course, Mom knows I don't listen very well." Juliet kicked off the floor, hovered in front of him, then literally flew down the hallway away from him. Apparently her need for the bathroom hadn't been that urgent after all.

Shawn muttered to himself and dumped the coffee down the sink. Well, there were worse things she could've put in there than a buttload of salt. He'd get her back for that later.

Shawn jogged down the hallway and reached the top of the stairs just in time to see Juliet skid to a halt and land with a plop on the first floor landing.

Across the living room stood Ara Park, Shawn's mother, her hands on her hips and her eyes flashing.

"Jules!" his mother snapped. "You know the rules about flying in the house!"

"I didn't break anything!" Jules wailed.

Shawn took deliberate, slow strides down the stairs. He came to Juliet's side and mouthed, "Serves you right."

She stuck her tongue out at him.

Seeing him, Mother's face softened. "Did you sleep well, dear? You had such a long drive yesterday."

"Never better."

A series of thumps and bumps drew his attention behind himself. He watched Ears gingerly descending the steps.

"I got your favorite cereal and the coffee is ready." His mother turned back towards the dining room. "I'm going to go check on my muffins. They should be almost done."

"Great. I could use a *good* cup of coffee." He eyed Juliet meaningfully.

She cackled.

Shawn and Juliet entered the dining room together. His father and Abigail, the second Park child and the only one who hadn't inherited her father's superpowers, were already seated, Abigail picking at her toast, her nose in a book, while Father sipped coffee next to a mostly empty bowl of oatmeal.

"Morning, Shawn," Father said.

"Hey, Dad. Abs." An array of cereal boxes stood in the center of the table along with a stack of bowls and a carton of milk. Shawn picked out one and dumped its contents into a bowl. "When did you get in?" he addressed his sister.

"A couple days ago. Soon as winter break started." Abigail was in her sophomore year of college and apparently doing very well based on everything his parents had told him.

"Cool." Shawn selected a spoon from the basket of flatware his mom had left next to the cereals and poured milk into his bowl before sitting.

For a while they ate in silence. Mother entered, offering coffee refills to everyone present and a new cup for Shawn. He said thank you.

"You aren't going to join us?" Dave Park asked his wife.

"Muffins aren't done yet," she said simply. She disappeared back into the kitchen.

Shawn took a bite of his cereal, glancing at Juliet across the table as she spooned copious amounts of sugar into her coffee.

"Have you applied to any colleges yet?"

Dad cast a sideways glance at Shawn's little sister who shook her head.

"Nope. I'm applying to DOSA next month."

Shawn's spoon dropped into his bowl. "Huh? Already? You're a kid."

"According to DOSA, I only need a high school diploma and to be over the age of eighteen. I wanted to wait until after Christmas, but yeah, I've already got two potential leads on DOSA teams looking for a rookie." She sipped her coffee. "What's the point of going to school and racking up thousands and thousands in debt when I know what I want to be?"

Shawn arched his eyebrows at his dad. "You're hearing this, right?"

"She's not a minor anymore, and chances are if I forced her to go to school, she'd just end up in DOSA anyway." Dad didn't even bother to sound disappointed. "She knows what she wants, and she's going for it."

"Yeah, but don't you think she'd have better career advancement opportunities with a degree?"

"Only if I want to go into administration someday, but I don't. I'd shrivel behind a desk. For the on-the-street villain fighting stuff I want to do, I've already got the qualifications." She aimed her palm at the empty end of the table and let off a puff of energy. A whiff of ozone tainted the room.

"Jules!" their mother shouted from the kitchen. "I smell that! What did I tell you about power blasts inside?"

"Sorry, Mom." Juliet then focused on Shawn again. "Even you didn't really need a degree. You're not going to go into paper pushing anymore than I am."

"Yeah, but I wanted the experience."

"Well, while you spent your four years getting 'experience' taking tests and writing papers, I'll be getting mine fighting villains and stopping crime." She punched one fist into the palm of her other hand. "Gonna have four years seniority over any sissy college boys who join the team."

"Hey, I've taken down villains too." Shawn frowned at his father. "You're really not going to back me up here, huh?"

"You've got the fancy college degree. Surely you can win a debate against a lowly high school grad." Father hid his mouth behind his coffee cup, but his eyes sparkled.

Juliet gave an unbecoming titter and high-fived her father across the table.

"I'm with Shawn," Abigail spoke for the first time, not even looking up from her book. "You and Mom would never have been this chill if I'd let my scholarships sit unused."

In spite of her taking his side, Shawn indulged in an eye-roll. She liked to bring up those scholarships every chance she got.

"You don't even have superpowers, though!" Juliet protested.

"Just super-intellect." Abigail gave a smug smile.

"Great, Nerd Girl. Can't wait to see you save the day with your stellar report cards." Juliet made a face.

"Are you saying a person can't have value without superpowers, Jules?" Shawn's mother slipped into the room behind his sister, carrying a basket of steaming muffins. A fragrance of blueberries and toasted sugar wafted from them.

Juliet flushed. "No, Mom."

"Good." Mother settled into the seat between her husband and younger daughter.

Shawn snickered to himself and picked out a muffin.

"When are you picking Katie up from the airport?" his father asked.

Shawn glanced down at his phone, resting on the table a few inches from his coffee cup. "She doesn't get in until noon, but I'll probably leave soon. Just in case there's traffic or something."

"Is she still going by Apparition for her hero handle?" Juliet asked.

"I hope not." Abigail shuddered. "That name is too ... yellow."

Shawn did not for one minute understand what that meant, but he figured if she could put up with him having the ability to fly and shoot power blasts from his hands, he could live with her claiming words had colors and colors had sounds, even if it made no sense.

When Abigail had been in middle school her synesthesia had been so strong she'd had to quit band class because she said the colors were giving her a headache. Since then it had either calmed or she'd learned to cope with it to the point that it just didn't come up as much. When she did bring it up, though, it still mildly baffled him.

"No, she agreed the handle was too yellow and changed it to Dreampainter." Shawn winked at his sister.

Abigail blinked at him.

"Kidding," he said. "Not about the handle change, though. Apparition reminded her too much of her time as a villain. Her father picked it out for her, and since she's joined the SVR, she's taken more ownership of her sable persona. I think it fits her."

"From what you've told me about her, I can see it." Abigail nodded. "It's very blue, but not bright bright blue. More periwinkle."

"Sure." Shawn tried not to laugh.

"Whatever color her name is, I can't wait to meet her." Juliet shot Shawn a toothy grin. "I have so many embarrassing stories about your childhood to tell her."

"Hey!" Mom frowned. "That's my job."

Shawn blanched. This could be torture. Maybe he should pick up Katie and flee the state with her.

"Can we give your brother a break?" Father said pointedly. "After all, I, for one, don't want him to be afraid to bring his romantic interests to meet us."

"Not our fault if he chickens out." Juliet narrowed her eyes at her brother. "Man up, dude. It's fair payment for when you gave my first boyfriend that, 'if you hurt my sister they'll never find your body' lecture."

"That's just my job as a big brother, and you're welcome for me looking out for you."

"Like I need protection." She aimed her fist towards the empty portion of the room before glancing at her mother and putting her hand down without any demonstration of superpowers.

Shawn took a sip of his coffee, holding it under his nose to savor the rich aroma. Yeah, pale blue fit Katie somehow. He could imagine her wearing that color really well, for one thing. Man, he couldn't wait to see her again. He also couldn't wait to put his plan into action for their future. Of course, he did want to talk about that with his dad first.

He turned his mug in his hands. It would be easier to find time to discuss it *before* Katie got there. It was hard enough to get private time with his parents and sisters in the house, and once Katie arrived, it would be torture to pry himself from her side for more than a minute.

Dave Park took the last sip of his coffee and picked up his plate. "Well, Mom cooked breakfast. Who wants to help me with dishes?"

"I can." Shawn shot out of his seat.

Everyone stared at him.

He coughed. "I ... um, I was hoping we could have a few minutes alone to talk anyway. Might as well multitask."

The women around the table exchanged glances, but

Father just nodded. "Gather up the dishes, and I'll meet you in the kitchen."

Trying not to make eye contact with his mother or sisters, Shawn collected a stack of dishes and brought it into the kitchen. His father ran hot water over a mixing bowl, rinsing muffin batter down the garbage disposal.

"You want to wash or dry?" he asked.

"Dry." Shawn placed the dishes on the counter and took up a towel.

"So what did you want to talk about?" his father asked a few dishes in.

Shawn considered his approach. He had every faith that his father liked Katie, but even Shawn had to acknowledge that her past as a supervillain and his career as a superhero complicated things—even if she was on the path to rehabilitation.

"Katie and I have been together for over a year now," he said.

"Yeah, I know. I was there when this whole thing started, remember?" His dad chuckled.

"I guess, but we haven't been around each other as much since I started with DOSA, so ... it's getting pretty serious, Dad." That seemed the easiest way to explain it.

"I kind of thought that might be the case when you asked if she could spend Christmas with us."

Shawn wiped down another dish and set it in the cabinet before deciding to just come out with it. "I'm going to ask her to marry me."

Dad put down his sponge and wiped his hands on a nearby dishtowel. He let out a long breath. "Can't say I'm surprised, but somehow I'm still not ready."

Shawn swallowed. "Do you think it's a bad idea?"

"No, not at all," Dad quickly added. "She's a sweet girl, Shawn. Whatever her past, there's a sincerity to her that I admire, but more than that, I can see how it would work with you. You're one of the most genuine people I know, and I know I'm your father so I am supposed to

26

think the world of you, but I mean it. You don't hold back, and you need someone who is willing to give as much to you as you will give to them. I think she's got that potential, and … I just hope you two are as happy as me and your mother are." He took a step towards Shawn, arms outstretched, but paused before Shawn could accept the hug. "Wait a minute. I need to talk to your mom about something. Is it okay if I tell her?"

"I guess—but not the girls, all right? Not yet, at least." Shawn winced. "I don't want them being all weird when Katie gets her. Jules, especially, won't be able to keep a straight face if she knows."

"My lips are sealed. Finish up here. I'll be right back."

Shawn nodded and concentrated on the dishes. Now that someone else knew, the idea seemed more like a reality, like something that *would* happen instead of something he simply hoped would happen.

A blissful calm settled over him. He was really going to do this. As long as she said yes, everything was set.

A smile quirked the corners of his lips, and his dish washing pace sped up.

He was already draining the sink when his father returned, Shawn's mother beaming at his side.

Shawn shifted uncomfortably. "He told you, I'm assuming?"

She tackled him in a hug. "Oh, my little boy has grown all the way up."

His face warmed, but he returned the embrace. "I guess I have."

She withdrew and glanced at Dad. He took one hand out from behind his back and held out a small box.

"The main reason I wanted to bring her in on this is that we talked about you having this someday." He opened the box revealing a diamond solitaire. "It's not the flashiest, I'll admit—"

"Oh, shush. It's beautiful." Mom pressed Dad's hand.

"Didn't stop you from swapping it out for that bigger

one I bought you for our twentieth," Dad teased.

She stuck her chin in the air. "An engagement ring only meant that I'd caught myself a superhero. Keeping him for twenty years without murdering him out of frustration? Now *that's* an achievement I want to show off."

"I can't take this." Shawn pushed the box away. "It's too much."

"Before you decide, let me tell you a little about this ring." Dad turned it around to gaze at it. "When your mother and I decided to get married, I was new to DOSA and my powers as a whole."

Shawn nodded. His father had told him the story of how he'd decided to undergo the genetic alteration that had awakened his powers as a young military officer.

"I wasn't making much and didn't have great standing in the agency yet. It was less friendly towards families back then. Higher-ups thought domestic entanglements would divide a hero's attention and loyalty and lessen their value. Thankfully, a few influential voices, like Allay, who had the committee's ear, did a lot to change that, but at the time I wasn't sure I could afford to get married at all let alone buy her a ring." Dad slipped his arm around Mom's waist. "Then one day, my team took a call for a jewelry store theft. I ended up being the one to recover the stolen items. Imagine me, a young DOSA agent, desperate to pay for a wedding and a new life, faced with a stash of jewels worth more than I'd make in a decade."

Shawn gawped. "You're not saying you stole it?"

"No." Dad laughed. "I'm saying that for the first and last time in my career I was very much tempted by the villain life, or at least pocketing something then claiming it hadn't been there when I'd found the rest."

"But he didn't because that's not who he is." Mom leaned her head against his shoulder.

"Only because I chose for it not to be, in that instance and in others throughout my career." His father squared his shoulders. "Life is full of places to screw up and take the wrong path, Shawn. Never grow so confident in your own righteousness that you don't remember that. If you do, one day a choice may blindside you and you'll make the wrong call before you even recognize that you're being tempted." He eased from his lecture voice to his normal, conversational tone. "Anyway, in this case, I got the best of both worlds to an extent. We're not supposed to take financial rewards from those we help, but I ended up befriending the owner of the store, and when he heard about my engagement, he cut me a deal and extended me credit. Said he trusted me to pay him back when I could, but not to worry about it until I could do so without hardship."

"How long did that take?" Shawn asked, fully confident that his father had long ago made good the debt.

"About five years," Dad answered. "To me, though, this ring represents more than just my love for your mother. It represents the hard choices a man has to make as both a hero and a father but also the rewards for making those choices."

"Well, now I *really* can't take it," Shawn said. "It's too much, Dad. Not the size or the value, I mean ... well, the value, but not the monetary value. Don't you want to keep this, Mom?" He turned a pleading glance to his mother.

"No, I don't." She took the ring box out of his father's hand and held it out to her son. "I have always loved the idea of an heirloom ring, but since engagement rings aren't a Korean tradition neither my family nor your father's had one to work with. So we start our own tradition. This will be our heirloom, and I want you to give it to your sweet little Katie." She took him by the wrist, turned his palm upward, and plopped the ring into his hand. "There. I won't take no for an answer."

He let out a breath. "This means a lot. I can't thank you enough."

"I take payment in grandbabies." She winked.

Shawn choked.

Chapter Four

One hand in his jacket pocket, clutching his phone, Shawn scanned the people exiting the arrivals section of the airport. Finally he sighted her, her red hair standing out across the room. He stood a little straighter, putting all his willpower into not vaulting across the airport in a single bound. That would *definitely* end up all over social media, and while DOSA didn't insist their sables maintain secret identities or hide their abilities, they did tend to get irritated at unnecessary grandstanding. Being the guy who literally flew across an airport lobby to pick up his girlfriend would at the very least get him ruthlessly mocked at work and at worst might be a mark against him in his future career.

Katie's eyes swept the space before her before they made contact with his and lit up. He waved, and she hurried towards him. The rolling carry-on suitcase she dragged behind her got caught on a security line stanchion which wobbled. Katie gasped, caught it, and disentangled herself before turning a vibrant shade of pink.

Shawn's whole being lightened.

Man, being that cute should be illegal.

They met each other halfway. Shawn hesitated, wanting to go in for a full kiss but uncertain how she'd feel about the PDA. Instead he wrapped her in a hug. Her arms surrounded his neck, her fingers working into his dark hair, and all sense of decorum crumbled. He lifted her off her feet, squeezing her for all he was worth.

"It's so good to hug you again," she said.

"Oh yeah." He gave a happy sigh before he released her. "Do you have any other luggage?"

"Nah, traveling light." Her eyes sparkled. "I brought

my new drawing tablet. You should see it. It's so much better than pen and paper. If I want to change something ... well, I'll show you later."

An elderly man hauling a carry-on that had to be pushing the weight limit swerved around the couple with an irritated grunt.

Shawn cleared his throat. "I think we're blocking traffic, and I parked in the short term lot, so we better get moving." He picked up her suitcase, retracting the handle so he could carry it rather than roll it along.

"Okay." She took his hand. "I can't wait to see your new truck."

"New to me," he qualified as they wove their way through the bustling airport. Piped in Christmas music played faintly over the murmur of holiday travel and the squeak of luggage carts. "It's nothing much to look at, but I've made a little bit of a side business helping my teammates move things—I get paid mostly in pizza."

She laughed. "Well, I don't even have a driver's license, let alone a car, so I'm still impressed."

Shawn briefly debated offering to teach her to drive, but with everything else he had planned for this all-too-short holiday visit, probably better not to push it.

They reached the short term parking lot, and he placed her suitcase in the cramped backseat of the extended cab.

She settled into the passenger seat as he started the engine. Her fingers twitched on her knees and vague images of flowers and birds flitted before her.

"Showing off your powers, huh?" He reached out and touched one of the birds, feeling the brush of feathers against his skin for a moment before the image faded out of existence. Katie's illusion powers were strong enough to fool multiple senses, a fact that meant they could be either fascinating or terrifying depending on how she used them.

She dropped her gaze to her lap. "It calms me."

"Are you nervous? Why?"

She shrugged. "It's a big deal, you know? Meeting your family. What if they don't … I'm a former supervillain. What if they don't think I'm good enough for their son?"

"You've already met my dad, and everyone knows your story." He reached over and rested his hand on her shoulder. "Trust me. They're going to love you, Katie. Just like I do … well, maybe not quite that much." He leaned across the center console and kissed her lightly on the lips. The warmth of her breath sent a wave of delight through him. "I have missed you so much." He brushed his fingers through her hair.

She gave a nervous smile. "I've missed you too— which sounds dumb. We just video chatted yesterday. It's not like we haven't seen each other in a long time, but yeah, this is better."

"So much better." He kissed her again. She pressed her lips against his before gently biting his bottom lip. He shivered and all his resistance broke. They kissed again and again.

Shawn's phone went off in his pocket. He jerked back. "Dang it."

She withdrew, face aglow. "We probably should get going anyway. Short term parking, remember?"

"Yeah. Let me see who this is, though." He pulled out his phone. "Huh, it's my team leader."

"You should probably take it then." She buckled her seat belt.

He answered the call. "Hey, Crystal. What's going on?"

"Are you alone?" Her voice sounded tense.

He glanced at Katie. She didn't seem to be listening, and his phone volume wasn't up too loud so she probably couldn't hear, but it was still weird that Crystal led with that.

"Uh, not really. I just picked up my girlfriend from

the airport, and we're heading towards my parents'. Is it work related? I can step out of the truck for a minute."

"No, don't ... look, Shawn, you're new to this life, and it's high stress, a lot of hard choices. If there is anything going on, you know you can come to me, right?" Her tension increased to full on desperation. "We all make mistakes, but your dad and I came up in DOSA together. I don't want you to ... if there is anything you need to tell me, any trouble you're in, you can be honest with me. We'll work through it. Okay?"

Shawn struggled to make sense of the words. "Is this about the Abounder case? I meant it when I said I was sorry for how that turned out. I know I have a lot to learn about working on a DOSA team. I don't want you to think I'm unteachable."

"No, that's not—" She made an exasperated noise. "Look, what I said, think about it, okay?"

"Okay. I will." His stomach twisted as the call ended without so much as a goodbye. "That was weird."

Katie's pale eyebrows melted together. "What did she want? Was she mad at you?"

"That's the thing, I don't really know." He thought back over the last few weeks. Other than the Abounder fiasco—which even with his willingness to take responsibility, he didn't feel was completely his fault—things had been going well. Had he messed up something without knowing it? Something with his paperwork? Something he'd said offhandedly that had given offense? Had one of his teammates complained about him? "She acted like she wanted me to come clean about something, but I can't think of anything I've done wrong."

"Maybe she's just being thorough," Katie said. "Rain does accountability check-ins with me *all* the time. Like, it always makes me feel like I'm in trouble, but she just wants to be sure my rehabilitation is going smoothly."

"But I'm not being rehabilitated."

"I know that." She frowned. "Doesn't mean you can't

screw up, though."

"I guess." He set the phone in the cup holder in the center console and turned the key. As he did, his elbow jostled against his other jacket pocket, the one where his mother's ring box sat. He let his eyes take Katie in, imagining her face being the first thing he saw upon waking up for the rest of his life. Was he really sure about this? Yeah, he was. Maybe he should've gone down on one knee at the airport. That sounded kind of romantic ... too late to go back, though, and he definitely wasn't going to be the guy who proposed in a parking lot.

He glanced at the clock. "You want to get something to eat? It's about lunchtime anyway, and I'd like a little time to catch up with you before we dive into the chaos of my family Christmas."

"I am a little hungry." Her face brightened. "Do you know any sushi places around here? My team introduced me to sushi, and I think it's my new favorite."

"Got it." He reversed out of the parking space.

Fifteen minutes later they sat at a small table with a rainbow roll and some spicy tuna the only thing between them. Expertly wielding his chopsticks, Shawn selected a piece with avocado on top and dipped it in the soy sauce.

"You're much better with those than I am," she observed, awkwardly pinching a piece of spicy tuna between two flimsy wooden sticks. She squeezed too tight, and the rice lost its structure.

"Spent a summer at my grandma's outside of Seoul when I was fifteen." He held up his chopsticks. "Though Korean chopsticks are usually made of metal. Much better as weapons."

"That's what I like about you. Always ready to throw down."

He reached across the table, scooped up some sushi for her, and held it out. She giggled as she ate it off his sticks.

She chewed and swallowed before saying, "You're

spoiling me."

"Good."

"Oh!" She pulled out her phone. "Mom wanted me to text when I landed, and I completely forgot. She's probably trolling news sites, checking that my plane didn't crash."

Shawn paused. He hadn't thought about Katie's family. Did he need to give them a warning before he proposed? Ask her mom for her blessing? How did that even work?

"Is your mom okay with you staying with me over the holidays?" he asked. "This is only her second Christmas since you two were reunited, so I feel kind of bad about monopolizing you."

"She's okay." Katie sent a text then set her phone, screen down, on the table in front of her. "She's got her other family."

Shawn nodded. Between when Katie's non-custodial biological father had kidnapped her as a young child and when she escaped his grasp at nineteen, Katie's mother had remarried and had two children, both of whom were still under ten. While Shawn had no doubt that Katie's mom still adored Katie, it had to be awkward, having an adult daughter with a weird, supervillain past introduced into her homelife.

"I'm sure she still wants you there, though."

"Yeah, she does, but she understands that me and you don't get a lot of time together, and I was there over Thanksgiving." She dipped a bit of pickled ginger in the soy sauce before popping it into her mouth. "She'll be okay."

They ate in silence for a few minutes before Katie spoke again.

"Ooh, I have something to show you!" She pulled a plastic case with a transparent lid out of her pocket. Inside Shawn could clearly see a set of white plastic earbuds. In spite of how standard these looked, eagerness brimmed from Katie's eyes. She slid her thumb along the edge of the case. Something clicked and the bottom of the case slid back to reveal six small silver disks, each about the size of a nickel. "Aren't they just adorable?" she all but squealed.

"Cute as buttons ... are they buttons?" He took a wild guess.

"No, silly!" She popped one out of the case and held it up. "These are my new trackers. Remember how I told you that Rain really appreciated my expertise in surveillance?"

He thought back. "A couple of months ago, right? You said she was going to develop some tasks and training around it, but I don't think you mentioned it again."

"Well, it's all very hush hush." Katie took on an exaggeratedly serious expression.

"Which is why you're squeeing about it now?"

"Oh, you're old blood DOSA. Rain wouldn't mind me trusting you." She put the tracker back in the case and the case back in her pocket. "I'm in charge of most of the team's recon now. Rain mostly trusts my instincts ... well, pretty much in everything except warrants. Those are pesky, and I still can't quite get my head around when it's okay to spy on someone and when it's not." Her nose wrinkled. "In the villain scene it wasn't that complicated."

"Yeah, privacy laws are such a pain." He chuckled.

She flattened the mound of wasabi on her now empty plate with the edge of her chopsticks and started tracing a design into it. After a moment, the green paste took the shape of a flop-eared dog.

"Hey, it's Ears!" He leaned closer. "I bet he's going to be happy to see you again too."

"I remember the first time I drew him for you," she said. "Seems like forever ago, even if it was only last year."

"A lot's happened since then." He reached across the table to stroke her hand.

Beneath the table, her toes found his calf, tracing up his leg.

Heat washed through him. "Do you want something else? I think they have green tea ice cream and boba tea on the menu."

"I wouldn't mind some boba to go, but I'm ready to rip off the Band-Aid and meet your family." Her foot withdrew.

"I promise they don't bite ...well, Jules, maybe, but the rest of them are pretty normal, at least as normal as a family can be with over half of its members having superpowers."

"If they were completely normal, I wouldn't fit in at all," she pointed out.

"Neither would I." He placed a few bills on the tabletop before standing. "Let's go then."

Chapter Five

Katie stared out the window of Shawn's truck until her eyes ached. They drove past perfect house after perfect house, places with swing sets in the yards, pretty hedges ... real family homes, the type she would've given anything to live in when she was growing up. She sank down smaller.

I don't belong with a family that lives in places like this. I'm too odd. Too broken. What will we even have in common? What do ordinary people talk about? What do they do for fun?

"Hey." Shawn's hand brushed against her knee.

If the seat belt hadn't been holding her in place, Katie would've hit the ceiling. Her powers went off, and a haze of smoke burst around her, obscuring her from view.

"Whoa!" Shawn hit the brakes. Katie jolted forward, and her illusions vanished.

"You startled me." Her gaze fell to her lap.

"Sorry." He eased off the brake. "I was just wondering what was going on in your head. You look like we're on our way to your execution."

She squeezed his hand. "Just nervous."

"Don't be. I promise, they're going to love you."

She bit her tongue. He didn't know that. He couldn't know that. Sure, Dave Park had been pleasant with her the one time they'd met, but he could've just been being nice. It didn't mean he was ready for her to be with his handsome, charming, intelligent, perfect son.

He tilted his head upwards. "Still pretty clear out. Weather is calling for cold but dry—I was really hoping for a white Christmas. Do you like snow?"

"I guess." She looked out the window again, barely listening to him.

"Here we are." He pulled to a stop in front of a two story house with brick on the bottom half and blue siding on the top. Her chest constricted. This was even more picturesque than she'd imagined. Her pulse hammered in her ears. She couldn't breathe.

"Easy, Katie." Shawn gripped her wrist. "Look at me, okay?"

She turned to him, her bottom lip trembling.

"We don't have to go in yet if you don't want to," he soothed, his dark eyes kind and sincere as always. "We can drive around for a while, go see a movie ... whatever you want."

The escape tempted her, but she shook her head. "No. It's not like it'll get easier if we wait longer. If they don't like me, though—"

"Shh." He leaned in for a kiss. She accepted his touch, relishing the warmth of his lips and the strength of his hand. "We've got this," he murmured. "If we can survive your dad literally trying to kill me, I think we can handle dinner with my parents."

She managed to nod but still cast a nervous glance back at the house.

A face peeked through the curtains in the front window.

She stiffened. "Someone's watching us."

He followed her gaze. "Dang it, Jules." His face lit up. "I owe her a prank. Do you think you could use your powers to, I don't know, make a massive rat appear in her bathtub tonight?"

Katie frowned at him. "I'm trying to make a *good* impression on your family."

"Oh, trust me. They know Jules well enough to know she probably deserves it."

Katie continued to stare at the house. Her powers swirled within her, and she longed to manifest them as a disguise or maybe a rock to hide under.

I want this. I want to meet Shawn's family because if

they are anything like him, they'll be wonderful. They have to be wonderful. Non-wonderful people couldn't raise a son like Shawn.

Shawn tightened his hold on her hand. "Let me know when you're ready."

"Now is fine," she said.

Shawn jumped out of the truck then walked around to open the door for her. She hopped out. A cold breeze pried its way under her jacket, so she zipped it up all the way to her chin. Shawn got her suitcase out of the back before offering her his hand. Together they walked up the brick path towards the front door.

The door popped open when they were only halfway down the walkway. A buoyant young woman grinned at them—the same woman who had been looking through the curtains, so Jules, Katie supposed.

"Is this Katie?" she asked.

"Nah. Katie missed her flight, so I just picked up the cutest girl I could find at the airport instead." Shawn winked. "Couldn't come home empty handed."

"You could've brought me home a guy then." Jules frowned. "I asked Santa for a new boyfriend for Christmas."

Katie laughed. "And here I just asked for art supplies. I didn't know boyfriends were an option."

"If you want, I can wrap myself for you." Shawn bent down to kiss her cheek.

"Ugh, no PDA!" Jules gagged. "Come on in. The rest of the family is hiding in the kitchen pretending they aren't super curious about what sort of girl was desperate enough to date Shawn, but I'm less proud." She stepped out of the way so Shawn and Katie could enter before giving Katie an appraising glance. "You're too pretty for him. What's the catch?"

Katie squirmed. "I think the catch is your brother, actually. At least, he seems like a catch to me."

"Quick witted too." Jules drew closer to her, suspicion

in her eyes. "Come on. You have to have a flaw—other than your obvious bad taste in men."

"Ease up, you idiot." Shawn fake-punched his sister's shoulder. He shuffled off his shoes, and Katie followed his example. "You said Mom's in the kitchen?"

"Yeah, apparently you bringing home a girlfriend means a special dinner." Jules rolled her eyes. "All my dates ever get is lectures about bringing me home before curfew and shotgun jokes. So much for gender equality."

Shawn put his hand to the side of his mouth and said in a stage whisper, "She's just sour because I'm the good child and she's the difficult one."

His sister stuck her chin at him. "I don't know if I'd brag about being momma's boy—"

"Juliet Yoonah Park!" A woman stepped through a doorway into the foyer. "Are you being rude to our guest?"

"No, Mom. Just to Shawn," Jules quickly said.

Mrs. Park gave her a stern look then glanced at Katie. Her expression softened, and for a moment Katie thought she was about to cry—which was silly. Why would seeing Katie make Shawn's mom emotional?

"You're Katie?" She rushed forward and drew Katie into a hug.

Katie tensed at the unexpected affection before something within her eased and she relaxed into the embrace.

"Yes, and you must be Shawn's mom? Mrs. Park?"

"You can call me Ara, dear. For now at least." Mrs. Park gave Shawn a knowing look. "We might work our way up to other titles eventually."

"So you're making dinner?" Shawn asked.

"Of course, but I can step away for a minute. Why don't you show her where she'll be staying and I'll make something warm for her to drink." Mrs. Park clasped one of Katie's hands. "You feel like ice! Do you want some hot tea? Coffee?"

"Tea would be wonderful, thank you." Katie nodded.

"I'll have it waiting for you in the living room once you've settled in." Mrs. Park bustled off as Shawn hefted up Katie's suitcase and motioned towards the stairs. There were four doorways off the main hall. He opened the second revealing a room with sky blue walls and posters of popular musicians on the wall—popular dude musicians.

"This is not your room, I'm guessing." Katie examined a set of perfume bottles on top of a vanity table.

"Uh, no." Shawn rubbed the back of his neck. "This is Juliet's room. She agreed to bunk in with Abigail while you're here. My parents—Well, they have house rules about where our 'guests' can sleep over."

The back of her neck heated. "Oh, I didn't mean ... no, this is fine. I'm sorry your sister has to give up her room, though. I could get a hotel, you know—"

Actually she couldn't. She'd lived in enough hotels moving around with her father that she had a general idea of what they cost, and her limited DOSA allowance wouldn't cover more than a few nights—plus since she couldn't drive she wouldn't be able to easily get back and forth to visit with Shawn. Still, it seemed wrong not to offer.

"No, you're fine." He set the suitcase on top of the dresser and looked around. "The bathroom is right across the hall. Um ..." He did a slow turn around the room. "I can't think of anything else, but if there's something you need, don't hesitate to ask."

"I'm sure I'll be fine." The air around her was pleasantly warm, so she slipped off her coat and laid it across the bed. She'd unpack later. "Your mom and sister seem nice."

He snorted. "Nice is not the word I'd use for Juliet, but my mom, sure. You want to go downstairs and get that tea or should I continue the grand tour of ... this?" He waved his hand around the bedroom.

"Let's go get some tea. I don't want to keep your mom waiting."

By the time they reached the living room, Mr. and Mrs. Park were sitting in chairs on either side of a lit fireplace. A jade tea set rested on the coffee table. Juliet sat cross legged on the floor in front of the fireplace and another younger woman—Abigail presumably—was on the ottoman next to a lit Christmas tree. Everyone in the family faced the conspicuously empty couch as if it were the centerpiece of the room.

A familiar hunger from her childhood gnawed within Katie. "You're a real family." The words slipped out before she could stop them, and her face immediately burned.

"Last I checked, anyway," Abigail said dryly.

Katie's blush flared, her face so flushed she could hardly see straight.

Dumb thing to say. Such a dumb, dumb ...

The clicking of dog claws on the hardwood floors interrupted her humiliation. Ears sauntered into the room, floppy ears swinging. He made a beeline for Juliet and plopped down with his head on her knee.

Shawn arched his eyebrow. "I see how it is, you traitor."

"You're the one who abandoned him. I just took over where you left off." Juliet stroked the dog's neck folds.

"Well, now that we're all here, why don't you sit down?" His mother stood. "I made that tea I mentioned." She poured a cup of steaming, yellow-green liquid. "Do you like sugar in it, Katie? Honey?"

"No, plain is fine, thank you." Gripping Shawn's hand, she settled onto the couch and accepted the cup of tea Mrs. Park offered her.

Shawn's phone chimed, and he shifted to pull it out of his back pocket. His brow furrowed. "That's weird."

"What?" His father leaned forward in his chair.

"Text from Crystal, my team leader, asking if I've

heard from Maestro—he's the puppeteering guy I told you about."

"Oh, yeah, the creepy one." Abigail nodded.

"I mean, his powers are kind of unnerving, but I don't mind the guy." Shawn unlocked his screen and stared at the text.

"Do you need to step out to call her?" Mr. Park asked.

"Nah." Shawn tapped his phone. "Just gonna let her know I haven't spoken to him since I left HQ. It's not like the two of us are close."

"You'd think your team leader would know that you're on vacation." Mrs. Park clicked her tongue.

"You know as well as I do that DOSA is lousy about personal boundaries, Ara." Her husband smiled at her.

Shawn stared at his phone for a moment. Katie hazarded a glance at the screen. For a second dots pulsed as if Crystal was replying but then they disappeared. Shawn grunted thoughtfully and tucked his phone away again.

"So, Katie, Shawn's told us you are interested in art," Mrs. Park said.

"I'm not sure if I'd call what I do 'art.' It seems a little presumptuous."

"She's being modest," Shawn broke in. "Her drawings are amazing."

"I have a lot to learn, though. I do love art as an admirer, even if I'm not quite where I want to be with my own skill yet."

Mr. Park nodded. "We should visit the museum together while you're in town—"

The family led the conversation in a pleasant direction, talking about things to do in Columbus, their Christmas traditions, and holidays past. Often Katie had nothing to add to it, but listening to them talk while Shawn kept his fingers entwined with hers lulled her into a sense of comfort. She liked being here. She liked these people. This wasn't the disaster she'd feared it would be.

After a bit, Mrs. Park stood. "I need to heat up the wok if we're going to have Japchae tonight."

A smile spread across Shawn's face. "Dang. Jules said you were making a special dinner, but I didn't know you were making that. You're in for a treat, Katie."

"I'm sure I am, but what exactly is ... what she said?" Katie looked to Shawn.

"Glass noodle stir fry. It's Mom's specialty," Abigail put in.

"And soon to be your speciality, too. You're going to help me make it. Both of you." Mrs. Park eyed Juliet meaningfully. "My grandma would roll over in her grave if she thought I was going to let the family recipe die with me."

"I can help too!" Katie stood up from the couch. Everyone looked at her, and her cheeks warmed. "I don't really know how to cook anything more complicated than eggs, but I'd like to learn."

"You're our guest, though—" Mrs. Park began.

"Trust me, Mom, she would rather be in there helping you than out here with me and Dad," Shawn put in. "Katie's a quick learner. I bet you anything she'll be better at julienning the vegetables than either Abby or Jules before the night's over. That is if Jules doesn't cut her fingers off and force us to spend the evening in the emergency room."

Jules stuck her tongue out at him.

"Oh, it's on," Abigail said.

Panic spiked within Katie. "Shawn's joking—but I do really want to help."

"Well, who am I to say no, then?" Mrs. Park's eyes twinkled.

Katie followed the Park women into the kitchen, and within a few minutes her world was alive with the smells of garlic, sesame oil, and rice wine. After a quick demonstration from Mrs. Park, she took over chopping peppers, mushrooms, and onions while the sisters bickered about how much sugar should go in the marinade.

After the ingredients were prepped, she stood back in awe as Mrs. Park cooked each one individually in her wok. Carrots first, then peppers, then beef, then mushrooms. The smells wafted around her, and her stomach growled. This might be even better than sushi.

Abigail and Juliet bickered constantly while they worked, but not mean-spiritedly. It almost seemed to be a game the sisters played, taking turns getting on each other's nerves or calling each other out for minor mistakes that probably didn't matter. Every time Ara Park would look at them, click her tongue, and say in a warning voice, "Girls."

It was so wonderfully ordinary. Not even TV family ordinary, but real, natural, and toasty warm.

This is a real family, and they've invited me in.

***

After dinner the Park family played cards. Katie had never played the game before—or any game really—so rather than try to learn she sat next to Shawn and watched him play. As the evening dragged on, she grew more comfortable, leaning against his chest as his arms circled her. He held the cards out in front of her so she could watch him play. It only took a few hands for her to recognize the patterns to the point where she probably could've played if she'd wanted to, but if she had, she would've had to give up her cozy spot pasted against Shawn. She really didn't want to do that.

He caressed her back and kissed the top of her head. Katie cast a quick glance at Juliet to see if she'd protest the "PDA," but Shawn's sisters were in the middle of arguing about some technicality involving the rules and didn't seem to notice. With a contented sigh, she shut her eyes.

"I think your guest is about to fall asleep, Shawn," Mrs. Park's kind voice said. "Perhaps we should call it a night?"

Katie jerked to attention. "Oh, I'm sorry. I'm not that tired, really."

Mr. Park folded his cards and set them face down on the coffee table. "I wouldn't mind turning in myself, but maybe we should talk about our plans for tomorrow first. It isn't often we get the whole family together these days. I feel like we should make the most of it. What do you want to do? I was thinking we could all tramp down to Santa's village—"

The siblings collectively groaned.

"What? You used to all love Santa's village!" Mr. Park protested, but from the light in his eyes, Katie suspected he was in on the joke.

"When we were six," Abigail said.

"I don't know. I seem to remember you begging to ride the reindeer when you were in middle school." Shawn teased his sister.

"Lies. Filthy lies." She tossed a piece of popcorn at him.

"I still have Christmas shopping to do," Juliet said. "Are you guys all done?"

"I've been done since Black Friday." Shawn stuck his chest out.

"You got everyone gift cards again, didn't you?" Abigail narrowed her eyes at him.

Shawn recoiled then mumbled, "Everyone likes gift cards."

"I'm mostly done, but I still need to get something for Katie," Juliet continued. "I wanted to meet you before I bought you something—because unlike Shawn, I believe gifts should be personalized, not just purchased." She scrunched her face at her brother.

Katie went rigid. She hadn't even thought about getting Shawn's family gifts. Was that expected? Were they all going to buy her stuff?

"I ... uh ... I have a few things left to buy," she said

quickly.

"It's decided then." Juliet hopped up. "Girls' shopping day tomorrow. Me, Abs, Katie—you want in Mom?"

Mrs. Park let out a breath. "I could use a few more stocking stuffers. What about Dad and Shawn, though?"

"Would they even want to go with us?" Abigail frowned. "Shawn's finished after all, and I know Dad only shops online."

Katie glanced from Shawn to his sisters. It did sound kind of fun, going shopping with the girls, but she didn't really want to leave Shawn for that long. "I'd like it if you came with us, Shawn," she said.

"Yeah, but I actually have something I need to take care of tomorrow, anyway." He leaned down and kissed her forehead. "I could meet you guys somewhere for lunch, though."

Katie's tension eased. That didn't sound so bad.

Mrs. Park stood. "Well, if I'm going to have to keep up with you girls all day tomorrow, I'm going to need my rest."

Mr. Park also rose, making a great show as if the action were difficult for him—which considering he could fly, Katie highly doubted. "If you kids decide to stay up, make sure you turn out the lights when you go upstairs, all right?"

"I'm turning in too." Abigail folded her cards and set them on top of the deck. "Want to do a little reading before bed."

Juliet lingered for a while before announcing that Shawn was boring company and she was going to go take a shower.

Shawn laughed. "So much for cards." He set his own cards down and pulled Katie even closer. She nestled in, feeling soft and warm and loved and ...

A yawn overtook her.

Sleepy.

"You tired?" His fingertip traced the bridge of her

nose.

"A little." She smiled apologetically. "I had to get up early for my flight, and I never sleep well before traveling."

"Big day tomorrow too." His hand slipped into his pocket, fiddling with something there for a minute. Not his phone—that was on the table. What did he have in there?

Before she could get too curious, he leaned in for a kiss. She yielded to him, her whole body melting.

"I wasn't lying when I said I have something to take care of tomorrow," he said as his lips parted from hers. "As much as I hate to say goodnight, we should probably both get some sleep."

Regret gripped her, but she pushed it down. She had two weeks to spend with Shawn, two perfect weeks. Still, everything within her longed to drag every moment of those weeks into an eternity. From Shawn's lack of attempts to rise, he wasn't any more eager than she was to end the night.

The mantle clock chimed midnight.

Almost simultaneously, Shawn's phone buzzed.

Katie pried herself from his arms. "Awful late for people to be texting you."

"Yeah." He checked his phone. "Huh. It's Crystal again."

"Still looking for Maestro?" Katie rubbed her eyes.

"No, Rick actually—that's Pleistocine's real name."

"She's lost the frost powered guy, too? By the way, I've been meaning to ask, did you ever ask him what his handle even means?"

"It's apparently an 'ice age' reference," Shawn explained. "I got an earful about paleontology when I brought it up. I guess it's an interest of his."

"Fun." She chuckled.

"He's actually a pretty cool guy." Shawn's eyes glinted mischievously. "Really chill. Like you'd think he'd give you the cold shoulder but—"

She lurched to her feet. "If you're going to keep making temperature puns, I'm going to bed."

"Didn't expect such a frosty reception from you." He pouted.

"You're an idiot, but at least you're cute." She reached down to jokingly ruffle his hair but somehow found herself sincerely running her fingers through it. Funny how that worked.

He stood and offered her his arm. "May I escort you home, madame?"

Suppressing giggles, she hooked her arm in his. "Definitely, my fine sir."

As they approached the door to her bedroom, her heart rate quickened. Even though she and Shawn had known each other for over a year and been a couple for most of that, their relationship had been mostly long distance. He'd managed a couple visits, one during spring break and the other right after graduation before his team assignment started, but with her still on probation at that point, she hadn't been allowed to stay outside of SVR headquarters past curfew—and apparently similar to Shawn's parents, her team leader, Rain, had rules about guests sleeping in the team quarters.

Katie had never dated before, let alone had a serious relationship. Shawn had briefly mentioned a high school girlfriend, but she'd never gotten up the gumption to ask if he'd been intimate with her—or when he would expect Katie to be intimate with him. It wasn't that she didn't find the idea appealing, but it seemed like so much to navigate.

Something a little braver than the rest of her crept out of hiding as they stopped in front of her door. She turned and leaned against it, gazing up at him with what she hoped were alluring eyes. "Do you want to come in for a little while?"

As soon as the words left her, discomfort raced

through her. What if he wasn't ready? Some people liked to wait for marriage. If he were one of them, would he think badly of her for the offer? Man, they should've talked about this over the phone at some point. That would've been so much less awkward.

Shawn's eyes widened before a look of longing crossed his face. Then his lips pursed, and he shook his head. "Man, I wish I could. House rules, remember?" He placed his hand on her neck, right below her ear, his thumb caressing her face.

"I remember. I guess I hoped I could tempt you a little bit." She played with his hair, not breaking eye contact as much as she wanted to shrink back and hide.

"Oh, believe me, I'm tempted." He kissed her forehead. "It's still my parents' house, though. Sorry I've got to be such a goodie-two-shoes killjoy."

"Don't be," she soothed. "I like that about you. Trust me, it only takes meeting a few guys in the villain scene before you don't want to so much as look at a bad boy ever."

Not that she'd ever dated any of those bad boys. Even when they had to work with other villains in the short term, her dad had never let anyone get that close, more out of paranoia than protectiveness, she thought. Still, the leering and the cat calls had been violating enough that she'd never been anything but repulsed by that type.

"I guess all that's left is a kiss good night, then?" She tilted her face upward expectantly.

He leaned into her, pulling her closer against his body as their lips met. She breathed him in. For a moment she savored the simple contact before desire flared within her and she deepened the kiss. Her teeth gently squeezed his bottom lip, and a shiver cut through him, vibrating into her. Their tongues touched, a strange but delicious sensation. He braced himself against the door with his right hand, his left holding onto her waist, tightening then loosening then tightening again in gentle pulses.

Katie ran her hands up and down his arms, appreciating the feel of his muscles beneath his long sleeved t-shirt.

A door opened, and Katie froze.

"Ugh, PDA! What did I say about PDA?"

Shawn groaned but didn't take his eyes off Katie. "If you don't like it, close the door."

"I need to get to bed anyway." Katie slipped out of Shawn's embrace and waved to Juliet. "Good night, Jules."

"Night, Katie, and you too, Lover Boy." Juliet batted her eyes at her brother before walking past them.

"I still owe you a prank. Don't think you're in the clear," Shawn called after his sister.

"Quaking in my boots. Not." She disappeared into a room down the hall.

Shawn focused on Katie, and his eyes softened. "Sleep well, okay?"

"You too." She brushed her fingers lightly across his hand. "I love you."

She shut the door behind her and closed her eyes to take in a few deep breaths. She was going to have great dreams tonight. She just knew it.

Chapter Six

Shawn was up early the next morning, but not earlier than his mom. When he got down to the kitchen, the room already smelled of hot coffee and baking muffins. Mrs. Park looked up from doing dishes and beamed at him.

"That girl of yours, Shawn! I didn't get a chance to say anything yesterday because I didn't want to embarrass her, but she's such a sweetheart!" She wiped her hands on a towel and reached for one of the mugs hanging from tiny hooks beneath the kitchen cabinets. "I guess you'd told me that, but I thought you were exaggerating."

"No, if anything I undersold her."

She poured coffee into the cup and passed it to him. "I do *not* understand how she could've been a supervillain."

Shawn's smile faded. "Well, that was her dad's fault. That man was a real piece of work." The memory of Katie's abusive father soured Shawn's mood. He sipped his coffee. "Do you need any help with that?" He nodded towards the sink filled with soapy water.

"No, I'm basically done. Why don't you go sit down until the muffins are ready? I'm sure the smell of them will bring your sisters downstairs soon enough."

Shawn took his coffee cup into the dining room and sat at the table. While he waited he fished his phone out of his pocket. If he was going to propose, he wanted to do it right. Not necessarily like a huge, flashy sort of thing— Katie didn't love being the center of attention, after all— but something memorable and romantic. Of course, he had to work with what was nearby. He pulled up a search engine and typed in "romantic locations near Columbus."

A lot of nice restaurants and ritzy hotels popped up. Over dinner might work, but it seemed kind of basic. The zoo might be cool ... or the Topiary Park, especially if it snowed.

The door opened, and his father entered. "Sleep well?"

"Well enough." Shawn glanced up from his phone. "How did you propose to Mom?"

"So glad you asked." Dave stuck his chest out. "Fourth of July on the waterfront. Fireworks exploding overhead, got down on one knee as the grand finale of the display went off. It was a work of genius."

"He says that, but the explosions were so loud I couldn't hear what he was saying." Both men looked up to find Ara Park standing in the doorway to the kitchen. "Took me half a minute to figure out why he was on the ground and looking at me instead of the fireworks."

Shawn laughed. "Well, as epic as that sounds, I'm not willing to wait until July to go through with this ... or even New Years for that matter. I'll be back with my team by then. I need something I can do within the next few days. Locally."

His parents exchanged a glance. "The Long Walk," they said together.

"That sounds ominous." Shawn frowned. "What is it?"

"On the campus of Ohio State, there's a small park with walking paths," his father explained. "The legend is, if a couple walks a particular path there, holding hands, then kisses at the end, their love will last forever."

"So kind of a magic spell, huh?" Shawn asked.

"More a tradition, all in good fun, but it's a sweet story," his mother said.

"Yeah, and Katie likes that kind of thing." Shawn pulled up a search engine and looked up the Long Walk. He read for a moment then whistled. "Dad, Mom, you're lifesavers."

"Happy to assist." Dad sniffed the air. "I smell coffee

and muffins, don't I?"

A strident beeping rose from the kitchen. "And you're just in time. Sounds like the muffins are done." His parents hurried into the kitchen.

Shawn tapped his fingers against his coffee mug. Now that he knew where he wanted to do this and to an extent how, he was eager to get right to it. Of course, his sisters had already claimed Katie for the morning. Maybe they could go after lunch. Should he bring flowers? No, he'd look stupid carrying them the whole walk without explaining why.

His parents returned, his dad holding a fresh cup of coffee and his mother a steaming basket of muffins.

"Mom!" Abigail wailed from the other room. "I can't find my new shoes."

Mrs. Park rolled her eyes. "If I can find them in thirty seconds, you're doing the dishes tonight."

"That's fine. Just help me. I'm desperate."

Dad laughed quietly as Mom left.

Shawn glanced around the room. "I'm kind of surprised Katie isn't up yet."

"She is, but your sister ambushed her," his father said between bites of muffin. "You've noticed your dog isn't around either, right?"

Shawn hesitated. "Uh, yeah, I guess I hadn't thought about it, but I haven't seen him since I woke up."

"It's been Juliet's job to walk him since you left him here. She was griping about how you should do it this morning because he's your dog. Katie volunteered, but Jules knew that Mom would never let her pass that off on a guest, so they compromised and went together." Dave raised his coffee to his lips. "I imagine she's telling embarrassing stories about you right now."

Shawn grimaced but shrugged. "Well, couldn't avoid that forever."

His phone went off. Unknown number.

Probably a telemarketer. He hovered his finger over

the button to reject the call then paused. The number was local to his team. With everything weird going on there he couldn't risk not answering. He swiped to answer. "Hey, this is Shawn."

"Shawn, it's me, Carl," said a masculine voice.

Confusion gripped Shawn. "Uh ... I don't know a Carl —"

"Maestro," the voice grew sharper.

Oh, duh.

Maestro was the only team member who preferred to go exclusively by his handle. Still, Shawn had been vaguely aware of his real name. He should've remembered.

Great, another strike against me.

"Sorry, this isn't the number I had you saved as." Shawn stood and walked into the kitchen, ignoring an inquisitive glance from his father.

"It's a burner. Look, I'm not in a place I can talk long, but I need to meet with you."

"Dude, I'm in Ohio, remember?" Shawn protested. "That's like a six hour drive. I'm sorry, but I'm not heading back to St. Louis just to—"

"You don't need to. I've been driving all night. I'm going to text you a map pin. It should be about an hour from you. Can you meet me there?"

Warning bells went off in Shawn's head. "What's this about? Crystal was looking for you last night."

"I texted Crystal. She knows I'm okay, but there's something important I need to talk to you about, not over the phone, in person. All right?"

Why me? Shawn didn't voice this though. He'd already strained enough of his team's goodwill.

This is strange, but Maestro is a team member. He's been with DOSA for over a decade. If he wants to meet there has to be a reason.

"I'll try to get away, but I really wish you'd tell me what's going on."

"I will. When you get here."

The line went dead. A moment later a text notification popped up. Shawn clicked on it and pulled up a map pin of what looked like a truck stop about an hour away just like Maestro had said.

Shawn walked back into the dining room.

"Everything all right?" his dad asked.

"Weird call from a teammate," Shawn explained. "I guess he's a couple hours from Columbus and wants to meet up."

"Why, though?" Dad asked.

"I don't know. It's kind of strange."

The front door opened, the jingle bells on the Christmas wreath clearly audible even rooms away. Ears gave a triumphant bark and happy voices chattered.

Shawn glanced through the dining room entrance into the living room where his sisters were now swarming Katie. If they really did intend to spend the morning shopping together, then he had a little bit of time to give to Maestro. He'd planned on using that time to figure out his plan of attack for the proposal, but with his parents' advice about the "Long Walk" he had his answer there. He shook himself out of it before sitting back down across from his dad. "I'm kind of the new guy on the team. I'm still figuring out the politics, but if he wants to meet up I'm sure it's for a good reason."

"Do you want me to come along?" Dad tilted his head to one side.

Shawn brightened momentarily but then thought better of it. Crystal had already accused Shawn of riding on Dave Park's coattails. If he brought his father along on team business, he'd never live it down.

"No, I'll be okay. It's only a short trip, and the girls have Katie's morning planned out for her, so I needed something to do anyway." He popped in an address for a restaurant near where the girls would be shopping and added it onto a route that included Maestro's meet up point. If he left soon he'd have plenty of time to get to Maestro and still make it back with time to spare before lunch.

It's all about balance. I can handle this. Some time for my team. Some time for my family, then some time for Katie and myself. I've got this. I'm going to prove to my team I'm a valuable member. Whatever is in store for me with Maestro, I'm not going to screw it up.

Chapter Seven

Shawn put the car in park in front of a boarded up gas station. He swallowed, staring at the decrepit building. Maestro's pin hadn't shown that the place was defunct.

This felt off. He picked his phone out of the cup holder and checked for messages. Nothing new from his team, but Jules had sent him several group selfies of her, Katie, and Abs trying on hats. He smiled. At least they were having a good time. He wouldn't want to be his mother, saddled with keeping tabs on that much feminine energy.

Other than his truck, the parking lot was empty, though he couldn't see behind the building. He pulled out his phone and texted Maestro's burner.

Hey, dude, I'm here. Where are you?

A few minutes ticked by with no answer. Based on the call, he had assumed Maestro would be waiting for him. That he wasn't here at all made the hair on the back of Shawn's neck stand on end.

As he watched, a motorcycle pulled off the freeway and came to a halt a few spaces away from Shawn. The rider was an average sized guy in a leather jacket and a black helmet.

That had to be Maestro. Shawn had seen the motorcycle parked in his team's garage a few times, though since the team usually used DOSA vehicles on missions, he'd never noticed who owned it.

Zipping up his jacket against the winter's chill, he put his hand on the handle of the truck's door but then paused.

Every instinct is telling me that something's off. If I don't listen to that, I'm an idiot. I need to take precautions.

He drew his powers into his hands and carefully projected a barrier of energy around his body. It wasn't full protection, but it would stand up to things like bullets. The air around him rippled gently as he slipped out of his vehicle and clicked the keyfob to lock the doors.

The motorcyclist stared at him—or at least faced in his direction. With the opaque visor, he could have his eyes closed for all Shawn knew.

"Maestro, is that you?" Shawn called.

The man removed his helmet revealing a familiar bearded face.

Shawn drew back. "Rick?"

"He called you too?" Rick set his helmet on his bike and took a step towards Shawn. His eyes flicked up and down his teammate.

"Uh, yeah, just a couple hours ago," Shawn said. "Do you think we should be looking for Crystal and Rapidz too?"

"I don't think so. When I left St. Louis they were both sleeping. They'd have to move fast to catch up."

Shawn mulled this over. For Rick to have made it there roughly at the same time as him, Maestro must've called him significantly before calling Shawn. Why hadn't Maestro mentioned that Rick would be there?

"Do you have any idea what this is about?"

"Not a clue." Rick pulled off leather riding gloves, black but coated with frost, more likely from his powers than the natural cold. "Maestro went MIA yesterday afternoon. Crystal was up in arms about it, but I'm not sure why. It's not like we had a mission or anything planned. She was so jumpy that when I got back from my jog last night, I found about six 'where are you' texts. Whatever Maestro's up to, it's got her stressed."

"Yeah, I got her texts. So he never reported in? He told me he texted Crystal when I asked if she knew what was going on."

"If he did, it was after I'd left HQ." Rick pulled a

61

smart phone out of his pocket. "Maestro called me in the middle of the night. Said he was in a jam then sent me this location. No explanation. No mention that you'd be here, but I kind of guessed you might be since he chose a place so close to where you were spending your leave."

"So why call us but not the rest of the team?" Shawn frowned. Maybe Rick had some sort of bro-code understanding with Maestro that if things went south they'd cut the female team members out of meetings, but no one had invited Shawn into that club.

"Your guess is as good as mine. I like Carl fine, but he's way closer with Rapidz than me. As much as I respect Crystal, she can be a little hard-nosed, so keeping her out of the loop, maybe I get that if he's really in trouble. Why he'd leave his girlfriend out of it but call in the new guy he's barely spoken to? Your guess is as good as mine."

Shawn blinked. Rapidz and Maestro were a thing? He really needed to pay more attention to the people around him.

The two men fell silent, occasionally checking their phones. Cars wooshed by on the interstate. After a few minutes one took the exit and pulled into the parking lot. It stopped on the other side of the defunct gas pumps.

Shawn stood a little straighter. The car was a generic gray sedan, about ten years old. Unlike the motorcycle, he didn't recognize it immediately.

"Is that him?" he asked.

"The car, I've never seen before," Rick murmured. "I'd think it would have to be him, though. I don't like this. Stay alert, kid. Okay?"

"Yeah." Shawn's power buzzed beneath his skin, rushing through his veins like adrenaline. The car door opened, and a figure in a ball cap and thick winter coat stepped out. Shawn's tension eased slightly, but he kept his powers at ready.

Maestro was in his mid-thirties and like most sables

athletically built. Dirty blond hair stuck out from under his ball cap. "Glad you two could make it."

"What's going on, Carl?" Rick jumped right into it. "You go no-contact with the team then wake me up in the middle of the night on my day off? I'm giving you the benefit of the doubt because you're a team member, but I'm this close to kicking your butt and dragging you back to HQ for Crystal to yell at."

"Easy!" Maestro held up his hands. "I'm sorry, but I really need help." His eyes darted wildly around the parking lot.

"So why cut out half the team?" Shawn asked.

"Because I don't know who to trust." Maestro's chin dropped towards his chest. "Look, guys, I screwed up. The bank mission, with Abounder—the guy got something on me. I can't go into details, but I was in a bind and made a bad call. Abounder found out."

Cold washed through Shawn.

"Crap," Rick muttered under his breath. "You're compromised?"

Maestro nodded.

Shawn glanced from Rick to Maestro. "How?"

"It's a long story, but I want out. I helped him with the bank heist because he promised that would make us even, but he didn't get what he wanted. The loot went missing. He thinks I took the diamond, but I don't have it. The thing is, if Abounder didn't get it and I didn't take it, someone else did."

"Someone meaning another villain or someone on our team?" Shawn asked.

"I don't think there was another villain there." Maestro shuffled his feet. "Crystal verified that the jewelry was in the deposit box when the bank closed for the night. After that, I had the building under observation the whole time. I hate to think it was someone on the team, but it had to be. One of us is dirty."

"So ... why did you call *us*?" Shawn asked. "How do

you know we're clean?"

"I don't, but you two are my safest bet. Rick because we've known each other for the longest and you for the exact opposite reason. You haven't been in the business long enough to be targeted. It takes time for the villain scene to break a DOSA agent down—at least it did for me." Maestro hung his head.

Rick and Shawn exchanged a glance.

Rick took a step forward. "Carl, I get that you're in trouble, but I know Crystal. There's no way she's dirty. You have to let me bring her in on this."

"If it's not Crystal, it's Rita, and maybe you're close with Crystal, but I'm way closer with Rita." Maestro's fists clenched. "I can't believe the woman I've been sleeping with would set me up like this."

"Are you sure it's one of the team, though?" Shawn pushed. "I know I'm the new guy, but I have a hard time believing a small time crook like Abounder would have the clout to turn *any* of us."

"It might not have been Abounder." Rick scratched at his goatee. "That diamond is a pretty big score. Like you find the right buyer for it, you're talking 'buy your own island and disappear set for life' money. That's a lot of temptation for anyone. Still, I hate to think any of us are that greedy—but I trusted Carl, so maybe I'm not the best judge of character." He narrowed his eyes at Maestro who seemed to shrink under his gaze.

"It was one mistake, Rick. I needed a little money to get myself out of a jam—"

"Then you should've come to me and asked for a loan, sold your laptop, taken a job delivering pizzas on the side, or I don't know, do anything but get into bed with a supervillain!" Rick barked. "Look, I like you, Carl, but I'm not covering for you. We're going to DOSA with this and we're going to get it cleared up the *right* way, got it?"

Maestro fell silent. Shawn's head ached. This was not the sort of situation he'd imagined himself caught up in

when he joined DOSA. DOSA sables were supposed to be
the good guys, like his dad. That his team had at least one
but possibly two members who had thrown away their
integrity for a quick payday ... dang, he didn't like this.

"Please," Maestro mumbled. "If Abounder catches up
with me, he's going to kill me. He thinks I've got the
diamond, and if I can't give it to him—which I can't
because I swear I didn't take it—he'll murder me. Maybe
I've messed up to the point where my career is a bust.
Maybe I'll even have to serve some jail time. I'll accept
that, but Rick—I am *not* ready to die."

Pity wormed its way into Shawn in spite of his best
efforts. "We've got to be able to keep him safe, don't you
think?" He addressed Rick.

"It'll be easier at HQ." Rick let out a long breath.
"Look, we think the rot is in our team, but our team isn't
all of DOSA. Shawn, your dad is Verve, the sable who
leads the Columbus branch, right?"

"Yeah, and he's solid," Shawn said. "I can call him—"

"What if our phones are bugged?" Maestro gasped. "If
it *is* Crystal, she has access to all our devices. If she hears
that we're bringing Verve and his team in on this—"

"We can drive straight to Columbus. Crystal is still in
St. Louis." Rick glanced at Shawn. "Can we take your
truck?"

Shawn nodded.

Maestro shuddered. "I don't like this. We can't trust
anyone in DOSA right now."

"We can trust my dad," Shawn said. "I know I'm
biased, but there's no way he's compromised, now or
ever. Besides, Abounder has never been active in Ohio
according to his file. There's no way he's got his hooks
into the Columbus team."

Maestro sighed. "I guess I don't have any better ideas.
Let me grab my backpack, okay?"

He started towards his car.

Not taking his eyes off Maestro, Rick lowered his

voice and addressed Shawn. "Look, he doesn't seem dangerous, but we can't trust him now."

"Agreed." Shawn scowled.

"I don't want you driving alone with him, but I also don't want to leave my bike here. You got anything I can use to secure it in the back of your truck?"

"I got the straps I used a couple weeks ago when moving that desk Crystal bought at a rummage sale."

"I can work with that." Rick crossed his arms. "Be ready. I don't think Carl is eager to go to Columbus. He might try something stupid."

Shawn's eyes widened. "Do you think he'll make a break for it?"

"If he does, you can bring him back, Flyboy." Rick smirked.

Shawn summoned his powers, hovering an inch or two above the ground. He and Rick moved to where the pumps were no longer obstructing their view.

Maestro slid into the front seat of the sedan. He glanced up, and a look of contempt crossed his face. A feeling like spider's legs on the back of Shawn's neck made his powers flare. He held his breath, though he didn't know why.

The sedan's door slammed shut.

"He's running!" Rick hissed.

The engine growled to life, and the car exploded in a ball of flames.

Chapter Eight

Shawn sucked in a breath and threw his powers in front of him. His shield collided with the onrushing shock wave from the car. Energy jolted up his arms pushing him backwards. He skidded across the pavement. Rick fell beside him as bits of ash and twisted metal rained around them. Shawn grunted and refocused. Debris bounced off his energy shield, keeping both him and Rick safe.

Ears ringing, he stumbled to his feet. Flames crackled over the blackened frame of the sedan. His heart sank. There was no way Maestro had survived that—was there?

He tried to run forward, but the heat buffeted him. The flames roared anew.

This isn't going to work. I need to put out the fire, not rush headlong into it.

He turned around to see his remaining team member sitting on the ground, gaping.

"Rick! Get up!" Shawn shouted. "I need your help. It's burning."

Rick stayed put.

Seriously? Had he hit his head?

"Your ice powers!" Shawn jerked his thumb at the fire. "They can put that out, can't they?"

Rick scrambled to his feet. He stood, staring down at his hands for a few seconds that felt like an eternity before stretching his arm forward and letting out a sputtering burst of ice. It shot out, hissing as it hit the blazing wreck that had been Maestro's car. A grin flashed across Rick's face. Seeming to get into it, he pushed both hands in front of him, his fingers shimmering with his powers. In a short time, ice coated the car like frosting, and the flames had died.

Shawn winced. Though the layer of thick ice obscured

the interior, he was more certain than ever that Maestro hadn't survived. Sirens blared in the distance. Glancing at the freeway, he could see several cars had pulled onto the shoulder to stare at the scene before them. One of them must've called the normie authorities. Shawn drew his phone out.

"We need to call DOSA."

Rick's hand clamped down on his arm. "Hold up."

Shawn recoiled. "Why?"

Rick let out a breath. "Look, Surge, remember what Carl said? About the team being compromised?"

"Yeah, but ..." Shawn struggled to get his thoughts in order. The car blowing up definitely suggested someone else was involved, someone willing to kill to keep Maestro silent, but that someone had to be in the villain scene. Shawn couldn't believe one of his teammates would kill.

Do I really even know them, though?

His stomach soured. "We can't hide this, though. What do you suggest?"

"We get our story straight. We don't know why Carl called us out here. He didn't have time to tell us much before he was offed. Let's say he said he thought someone was after him, but not that he thought that it was a teammate."

Shawn tried to keep up. "What do you think that will accomplish?"

"We can't be sure who did this. If we go to Crystal about it, and it's her, we're going to be next." Rick jerked his head towards the swiftly melting combination of burnt car and ice.

"But we were just saying that DOSA as a whole isn't compromised. We can go to my dad."

"As soon as DOSA knows, Crystal will know, and probably Rapidz too. The department isn't subtle enough to hide an internal investigation." Rick's hand brushed up against his chin, and he started scratching his beard as if it itched horribly. "Give me a day. I want to see if I can figure out who I can trust. Once I know for sure who is behind this, we'll take action, all right?"

Shawn didn't like this, but Rick had over a decade more experience dealing with DOSA than he did. If he said that was how it would fall out, he was probably right.

"We should at least tell them Abounder was possibly involved," he said.

"Yeah, we can do that. So this is the story: Carl called us here, but didn't say why. When he got here he was acting off, told us he was being hunted and that Abounder was after him. When we suggested we get him into protective custody, this happened. We clear?"

Shawn mulled over this. None of that was exactly a lie, but he still didn't like it much. "I guess, but only twenty-four hours, Rick. If it goes longer than that, I want to tell my dad. Maybe DOSA as a whole is a bad idea, but we can trust my dad. He knows people. Knows how DOSA ticks."

"Twenty-four hours should be enough." Rick released Shawn. "Make the call."

Shawn dialed in the DOSA emergency line. The operator gave a twenty minute response time until the clean up team arrived. Shawn's chest tightened. Would that team be his father's team? Columbus was the closest DOSA branch.

Easy, Shawn. That's not how it works.

Even with his admittedly limited experience, he knew that DOSA clean up crews were normally specially trained normies rather than the sable teams themselves. If there was a chance of villain involvement, a few sables might show up for security, but things like evidence gathering and taking witness statements were usually not the business of the actual teams.

Sirens grew louder and lights flashed in the distance. Rick fished in his pockets before drawing out his wallet. "Let me talk to them." He pulled out his DOSA credentials and stepped away from Shawn.

Once the first responders found out DOSA was involved, they left Shawn and Rick pretty much alone, instead verifying that Maestro was, in fact, dead and taping off the scene. With the intensity of the situation fading, Shawn quickly chilled. He paced up and down, rubbing his arms. Rick stood a little ways from him, fiddling with his powers to pass the time, summoning frost and ice in various shapes like a child playing with playdough.

A feeling of unease crept through Shawn. Had Maestro given any warning signs about being in trouble? Had there been anything Shawn could have done to save him? If he'd moved a little faster, could he have extracted his teammate from the car before the flames consumed him?

No. He probably died in the blast. Once that went off there was nothing anyone could've done, superpowers or not. Before it went off, though. Did I miss something? A click, a beep, a giant clock counting down to zero?

As much as he knew he couldn't have stopped it, guilt and regret chewed at him. Letting down his team on a mission was one thing. Allowing one of them to die—so much worse.

By the time the caravan of black DOSA SUVs arrived, Shawn just wanted to go home. He texted Katie saying he'd probably miss their lunch date. Proposing that afternoon was also definitely off. He didn't want his romantic story to include, "Well, I'd just gotten back from seeing a teammate incinerated before my very eyes—"

Poor Carl. Whatever he'd gotten himself into, he didn't deserve that. No one does.

Regret over never taking the time to get to know Maestro rippled through him. How would Rapidz take it? Especially if they were really a couple? Of course, there was a chance she was the one who had orchestrated his death. Shawn's stomach sickened at the thought.

Black suit wearing DOSA agents separated Shawn and Rick and transported them in different cars to a nondescript office building. Shawn tried to remember exactly what he was supposed to say and what he was supposed to hold back. It had seemed so simple when Rick had outlined it, but under the scrutiny of the clean up team, sweat beaded on the back of his neck.

By the time they were done with him, Shawn felt he'd gone over the story a dozen times. It was probably more like three, but they kept asking him to repeat things, backtracking to ask questions about things he'd thought he'd already addressed.

I'm not cut out for subterfuge, he thought wryly.

His stomach grumbled. His phone buzzed in his pocket, probably one of his family members or Katie wanting to know what was going on. The explosion had probably made the local media by now. If DOSA involvement was publicized, his loved ones would put it together that he had been there. He should've included "I'm safe" with his text about missing lunch.

He slipped his hand into his pocket and glanced up at his interrogator. "Look, if we're going to be here much longer, can I call my family? I don't want them to worry about me."

She shuffled some papers. "We're almost done, Mr. Surge."

Shawn arched an eyebrow. While it was professional courtesy to call a sable by their handle instead of their given name, he'd never come across the combination of handle and "Mr." before.

The interrogator glanced at the mirror lining one side of the room. Probably two-way, Shawn was assuming, if only because that was how it worked in police shows on TV.

Man, I never thought I'd be on this side of the table.

The woman stared at the mirror as if she could actually see through it. From her expression, Shawn

suspected she was getting instructions through the
earpiece she wore.

"Are you staying in the area?" she then asked.

"At my parents' ... my father is Verve. From the
Columbus team?" He hoped that would buy him some
trust points. Of course, with how Crystal reacted to him
being a legacy sable, that wasn't a guarantee.

"We may be in contact." She pushed the papers into a
manilla folder and stood. "You're free to go for now. I'll
have an agent escort you back to your vehicle."

Shawn left the interrogation room and walked down
the hall into the lobby. His breath caught in his throat.
Across the room, Rapidz and Crystal stood, staring at
him. Both women had haunted looks in their eyes, and
from the state of Rapidz's eyeliner, she'd been crying.
Shawn's chest ached.

Wanting to offer his condolences, he took a step
towards them.

"Surge?" A man's voice interrupted him.

He looked over his shoulder as another agent
approached him.

"Are you ready to go?"

"Just a—" Shawn glanced in the direction of his team
to find another agent leading them into the back.
Opportunity missed there. "Yeah, sure. Let's go."

By the time Shawn pulled up in front of his parents'
house, the sky was dark and the Christmas lights were on.
He put the truck in park and rested his head against the
steering wheel for a moment. His stomach growled. He
probably should've stopped to eat on the way home, but
he hadn't really felt like fast food, and he didn't want to
take the time to stop at a sit-down restaurant. Hopefully
his mother would have dinner ready soon.

He walked up the path and opened the front door
without knocking. He paused.

His family stood in the entryway, forming a half circle
blocking his way into the house. Their eyes searched

him.

"Um, hi, guys. I'm all right, really," he assured them.

Katie broke from the group and threw her arms around his chest. "When I saw the news alert about the explosion, I knew it somehow involved you. I just knew. Oh, Shawn. You could've been killed."

Sinking into her embrace, Shawn rubbed her between the shoulder blades. "I wasn't though. Me and Pleistocene are both unhurt. The explosion only reached Maestro."

She tightened her hold on him.

"HQ filled me in. I'm sorry about your teammate," his father said. "Even with the short time you've been on the team, I know that that can be a hard loss. If you need to talk to someone, I'm here, all right?"

"Thanks, Dad. Maybe later. Right now it doesn't feel real yet."

Katie released him, so he kicked off his shoes and made sure the door had latched behind him. Ears pushed his way through the family and sat at Shawn's feet, tail thumping on the mat.

Shawn stroked the dog's neck folds. "It's got to be rough on my team as a whole, though. They'd all worked with Maestro for almost a decade."

Guilt twisted at his soul. Should he be with the rest of his team right now? What sort of a teammate was he for abandoning them when they were going through this? As much as he hated to give up his vacation, his time with his family, and his chances of seeing Katie in person for a little longer—to say nothing of proposing—maybe he belonged in St. Louis.

Before he could voice this concern his mother swept forward, hugged him, then ruffled his hair. "I'm going to get you some beef bone soup."

His stomach rumbled in response. Mother slipped away, followed by Abigail.

Juliet snorted. "We should have you home more often. She's cooked more in the last two days than she has all month."

"I think that has more to do with our other guest than it does with Shawn." Dad flashed Katie a knowing smile.

She flushed pink and dropped her gaze to the floor. "I hate to make more work for her, but I've enjoyed learning from her. My dad never taught me how to cook much more than box macaroni and oatmeal packets. I didn't even know you could make soup from bones. I just assumed you threw that part out or gave it to dogs or something."

"You're in for a treat tonight." Shawn brushed her cheek with the back of his hand.

"Oh, I know. I've been sampling and smelling as we go." She beamed at him for a moment before her smile faded. "I'm so sorry about today, but I'm glad you're safe."

"I'm glad too." He bent down for a kiss. For once Juliet didn't react to it, walking quietly out of the room instead. Shawn entangled his fingers in Katie's hair. The loss of Maestro had stopped him from thinking how close he'd come to dying. If he'd gone to the car with Maestro or been standing a little closer or hadn't thrown up his shield in time to avoid the shrapnel, it could've been his family mourning him tonight. He held Katie closer. He did not want to die before he had a chance to make her his wife. Yeah, his team needed him, but his family did too.

Chapter Nine

Shortly after his return, Katie unwillingly pried herself away from Shawn to check on Ara Park in the kitchen. A massive stock pot bubbled away on the stove, filling the room with delicious aromas. At the kitchen island, Ara stood, chopping up scallions while Abigail took out bowls and Juliet fetched spoons. Another, smaller stock pot sat on the second burner. Katie peeked into this and found more bone broth, just starting to steam.

"Why so much?" she asked.

"That pot I took out of the freezer," Ara explained. "The new batch won't be ready for another couple of hours."

"Mom always keeps a huge supply of this stuff on hand, just in case," Abigail explained before dipping out of the kitchen for the dining room.

"Jules, would you start some rice?" Mrs. Park asked.

Katie's eyebrows melted together. "Then why did you make more if you had it already?"

"I wasn't going to, but when I said we were having it tonight, you seemed so excited to see how it was made. I didn't want to disappoint you by simply thawing some." Mrs. Park smiled softly. "Besides, it will get used up eventually. Like Abs says, we always keep it in the freezer, just in case."

Katie's insides warmed. "You're so kind to me. I don't know how to pay you back."

"I'm paid back every time my son looks at you and his eyes light up." Ara swept the scallions into a bowl.

Abigail returned. "What else, Mom?"

"Grab some kimchi, and then we just need to wait for the rice." Ara clicked her tongue. "I should've started that sooner, but I was so worried about your brother. This

DOSA nonsense is going to drive me to an early grave. I'm not sure how I'm going to cope when your sister joins too."

"Don't worry, Mom. You'll still have one child smart enough not to go risking her life flying around like an idiot." Abigail stuck her chin in the air. Juliet made a face at her.

Soon the family sat around the table, each with a steaming bowl of bone broth in front of them. Katie observed for a moment as the Parks dished up rice, kimchi, and other sides before doing the same.

The family fell silent. Unlike the previous night where they chatted merrily over dinner, the mood was subdued. Katie sneaked her hand under the table to squeeze Shawn's knee. He rested his hand on top of hers but didn't take his eyes off his meal.

The family was starting to clear away dishes when the doorbell rang. Everyone exchanged a glance.

"I've got it." Dave Park stood and left the dining room.

Katie's chest tightened. Though she didn't know why, she suddenly had a desire to run—well, to grab Shawn and run.

Pushing aside her instinct to help with dishes, she eased out of the dining room and stood at a distance to watch Dave answer the door.

"Crystal? I wasn't expecting you," he said. "I'm so sorry to hear about your team's loss."

Katie stiffened. What was she doing here?

Shawn came up from behind Katie, his face drawn.

"Sorry to interrupt your evening, Verve, but I believe your son is staying with you." The woman stepped around Mr. Park and scanned the room before making eye contact with Shawn.

Shawn started forward. "Hey, Crystal. Are you doing all right?"

"As well as can be expected." She frowned at him.

"I've gotten permission from DOSA HQ to run the investigation of Maestro's death. Unfortunately, there are a few details that aren't lining up, and I need you to come with me so we can go over things again."

Shawn's shoulders slumped. "Okay. I mean, I don't have much more to say beyond the statement I already gave, but I'll do my best to help."

Panic spiked within Katie, and she rushed to Shawn's side. "Can I come with you?"

"That's probably not a good idea." Shawn kissed her forehead. "Hopefully I won't be too late."

"Okay." She didn't like this. This was wrong. She couldn't put her finger on why, but she didn't want Shawn to go alone.

"I need to grab my coat. It's up in my room," he said.

"I've got it!" Katie burst out. Before anyone could question her, she darted up the stairs. Reaching Shawn's room, she paused and pulled her case of trackers out of her pocket. She took Shawn's coat from the hook on the back of his door and slipped the small metal disk into one of the pockets, zipping it up carefully so it wouldn't fall out. She hesitated. Her father had raised her to be paranoid, to put little faith in anyone but herself—and at the time himself, though in hindsight she knew he hadn't deserved it. Was she reacting from that old mentality now? After all, Shawn's team was DOSA, the good guys. Shawn would be safe with them.

Right?

Doesn't hurt to be sure.

She hurried downstairs, leaving the tracker in place.

Shawn stepped towards her as she approached and claimed his coat. "Thanks."

"Be careful." She avoided Crystal's gaze. Even if she didn't trust Shawn's team leader, she didn't necessarily want her to know that she didn't.

"I'm sure I'll be back in an hour or two." He kissed her cheek before casting a confident smile first at his dad then at his sisters and mother who stood in the doorway to the dining room, staring at him. "Don't wait up for me, though."

Oh, I will, Katie thought but stayed silent. Instead she reached up and lovingly brushed his hair back behind his ear.

As the door shut behind Shawn and Crystal, dread settled over Katie.

He has to be all right. If he's not, I don't know what I'll do.

***

Just because of proximity, Shawn expected Crystal to take him to the Columbus team's HQ, a building he was intimately familiar with, having spent a lot of time there as a child, following his dad around. Instead, however, she kept driving until they arrived at the same office building he'd been interrogated at earlier that day.

Once there she led him into one of the interrogation rooms and motioned for him to sit down.

"I'll be right back," she said simply before leaving.

Shawn unzipped his coat and fiddled with his phone. After about five minutes, Crystal returned, her face stoic. She placed a tablet on the table in front of him, displaying a photograph of a desktop computer.

"Do you recognize this?" she asked.

"Uh, it's a computer." He squinted at the picture.

"Just a computer?" She tilted her head to one side.

He caught sight of a sticker on the side of the case: *College City University*. He sat up straighter. "My computer, I guess. Why?"

She swiped her finger across the screen, and the tablet changed to a new picture: his computer case opened up to reveal the components and what appeared to be a clear plastic bag stuffed with cash wedged in along with them.

"How ..." His gaze shot from Crystal to the image and back again. "This has to be some sort of joke, right? When did you take these?"

"Yesterday morning." She pulled the tablet away. "After the mission went wrong, I knew something was off. Villains think they're sneaky, but they're obvious. They have playbooks. Compromising a DOSA agent with bribery is thankfully rare, but it happens enough that when something goes catastrophically wrong, I take a hard look at my team. Abounder wasn't working alone."

"He was working with Maestro!" Shawn protested. "He flat out told me and Rick that he was being blackmailed by him. Ask Rick. He can back me up."

"Rick told me about Maestro, but he also told me Maestro thought someone else on the team was compromised and had made off with the diamond. Information you conveniently left out of your own testimony."

Cold washed through Shawn. "Rick told me he was going to take care of that. I trusted him."

"I trust Rick too," Crystal said. "But it's trust with verification. I searched his quarters as well, along with Rapidz and Maestro's. This—" she tapped the tablet, "—was all I found." A look of pain crossed her face. "I should've brought you in right then and there. If I had, maybe Carl wouldn't—" Her mouth clamped shut, and she shook her head.

"That was why you called me at the airport?" Shawn breathed. "You thought ... Crystal, I swear, I have no idea where this came from. I wouldn't even know how to approach a supervillain—"

"Considering that you're dating one, I find that hard to believe."

Irritation rose within him. "First off, Katie's reformed —"

"This isn't about your girlfriend, Park," Crystal snapped. "I'm giving you the benefit of the doubt that the bomb was planted by Abounder, not you, which is why I'm still willing to deal here, but we know from Maestro's own confession that neither he nor Abounder took the diamond. That means there's a third person involved. If you want a chance to see the outside of a cell in the next decade, tell me where it is."

"I don't have it!" He drew back in his chair. This couldn't be happening.

"Did you sell it already? Is that where you got the cash?"

"I've never seen that money before. Someone is trying to set me up."

Rick. It has to be Rick. Why else would he tell me to be quiet about the team being compromised then mention it in his own interrogation? If I suggest that now, though, it will look like I'm trying to get out of this. I have no proof beyond that, and it's my word against his.

"Look, all I've ever wanted to be was a DOSA hero. Why would I throw that away six months into my first assignment? Maestro did say he thought someone else on the team was compromised. I'm sorry I left that out, but I didn't know who to trust. If it's not me, it's another team member which means the rest of us are potentially in danger—"

"I can look after myself." She squared her shoulders "Besides, I trust Rick and Rita more than I trust you."

"You trusted Maestro too," Shawn retorted.

"To an extent. I knew he had money troubles. I've bailed him out a few times throughout our acquaintance. When he went AWOL yesterday, I was willing to give you the benefit of the doubt, that maybe it was all Carl and he'd just used your belongings as a convenient stash place that wouldn't draw attention to himself—but him blowing up kind of verifies that someone else is involved here." She folded her arms over her chest, tapping her fingers against the opposite arm.

Shawn's chest tightened. "Maybe I should ask for a lawyer."

"Why?" Crystal's eyes sharpened. "Do you have something to hide?"

"No, but if you'd asked me fifteen minutes ago, I would've said there was nothing stashed in my computer case either." He hardened his tone. "Yeah, definitely a lawyer."

"I'll see what I can do." Crystal picked up the tablet. She put her hand on the doorknob then paused and looked back at Shawn, her gaze sad. "For your father's sake, don't draw this out. It's going to be hard enough on him as it is. If you meant any of that garbage you spewed about wanting to live up to your dad, come clean. End this before it gets any worse."

Shawn's tongue stuck to the roof of his mouth. Before he could even think of a reply, the door shut behind her, leaving him alone.

This can't be happening.

Shawn pulled out his phone. Should he call his dad? Try to explain what was going on? Or just wait for a lawyer? From what he could tell, he wasn't under arrest yet, but the situation seemed to be headed in that direction.

He stuck his phone back in his pocket. No point in worrying his dad. This had to be a horrible mistake. Shawn hadn't done anything, and any investigation would exonerate him. The money was a fluke. Yeah, it looked suspicious, but it didn't prove anything.

This will blow over. I haven't committed any crimes, so I have nothing to hide. I can't panic. Panic leads to stupidity, and I need to be smart here. Come on, Shawn, you can be smart, right?

Time passed slowly. He checked sports scores and news on his phone. The local media had several articles about the explosion, but they were thankfully vague. No mention of him being present, let alone a suspect. If only he could prove his innocence before it got to that point. Once the press got a hold of the story, his reputation might take a permanent hit, one that could stick around even after he was cleared.

The door opened, and Crystal entered again, this time accompanied by Rapidz. Rapidz's lips curled in obvious contempt. Remembering that she'd been involved with Maestro, Shawn cringed.

She thinks I killed her boyfriend. Man, even if I do get out of this, how am I ever going to repair things with my team?

"We're transporting you to the Columbus HQ. There's a holding facility there, and DOSA is sending an attorney to meet with you—unless you have your own you'd rather they contact?" Crystal waited for an answer.

Shawn paused. Did he? He'd never had a need for a lawyer, but his father might've. Maybe he had someone he'd want Shawn to use. His father would soon know what was going on anyway. Once they got to the Columbus HQ, his father's team would hear about it, and they'd definitely tell his father.

Man, I'm so grounded. In spite of everything, the thought twitched his lips into a brief smile. Rapidz's glare intensified, and he forced his expression stony again.

He stood. "No, I guess I don't. Let's get this over with."

Crystal reached into her jacket pocket and pulled out a coil of metal.

Shawn's face fell. *Disruptor cuffs?*

"Do you have to? I'm not a flight risk. I swear. My whole life is here."

Crystal's expression grew more severe. "Are you going to fight it?"

"No, ma'am." Shawn stepped around the table. Crystal slapped the coil in place around his ankle. Immediately his powers fizzled, the consistent humming energy that had accompanied him throughout most of his life sinking into his core where he could no longer reach it. He swallowed, trying not to dwell on the loss of part of his being.

"Let's go," Rapidz growled. "I want to get him off our hands as soon as possible."

Shawn's mind churned over everything as they walked through the building. He still had his phone. He hadn't been read his rights. That meant he wasn't under arrest yet, didn't it? Of course, the disruptor cuff seemed to suggest otherwise, but that could simply be a precaution. Sables were dangerous to deal with, and while both Crystal and Rapidz were more experienced, Shawn's powers were arguably a level above theirs. The only team member who had honestly made him even a little intimidated had been Rick, and for whatever reason, he was nowhere to be seen tonight.

A black DOSA SUV waited for them in the parking lot, a suited agent in the driver's seat. Rapidz opened the door to the back and gave Shawn a shove.

"Easy!" He held up his hands. "I'm not fighting."

"I wish you would." She sneered at him. "Give me an excuse to punch your lights out, Flyboy. I dare you."

He balked. "Look, Rita—"

"Shut up." She shoved him again.

Not wanting to get pushed into a fight, Shawn hurriedly entered the car.

Crystal climbed into the front passenger seat as Rapidz settled next to Shawn, still glaring at him. The SUV eased out of the parking lot and onto a dark road glistening in the streetlights.

This is going to be a long night. Maybe I should text Dad. Even if HQ will tell him, he deserves to hear it from me. He fished in his pocket.

"What are you doing?" Rapidz's hand shot out, much faster than Shawn's eye could track. She snatched the phone out of his grasp.

"I was going to text my family. Let them know what's happening," he explained.

"DOSA will take care of that." She slipped the phone

into her pocket. "For all I know you'd get a signal through to your supervillain friends to come and save your worthless—"

"What the—?" The driver slammed on the brakes and the horn simultaneously. Tires screeched. Shawn's head jerked forward, bouncing off the back of the seat in front of him. He grunted and twisted to look out the front. A hooded figure loomed in the middle of the street before them, twice as tall as an average man and growing.

Abounder!

"Oh crap!" Crystal flickered out of sight, her powers activating and cloaking her in invisibility.

"We've got this!" Rapidz reached for her seat belt.

Abounder leaped forward, growing as he moved. His hand surrounded the SUV as if it had been a child's toy. Shawn's head hit the ceiling, his jaw clicking painfully, as the SUV left the road. His powers flared within him only to be pushed back down by the disruptor cuff. The world toppled end over end over end. Shawn gripped the seat beneath him. Then with a crash and the shattering of glass, all went still.

Hanging upside down from his seat belt, Shawn's vision swam. Had he hit his head or was he just dizzy? He managed to unbuckle. His body crashed onto the car's ceiling beneath him. Shards of glass like sharp pebbles bit at him through his coat.

"Crystal? Rapidz? Are you two okay?" he asked.

Rapidz moaned. The driver swore. Shawn couldn't make out Crystal, either still invisible or flung from the car.

He crawled through the busted window. A giant hand shot out and grabbed him. Something pierced the skin at the back of his neck. A rush of stinging cold flooded his veins. The world wobbled, and all went black.

Chapter Ten

Sound echoed about Shawn, voices, the scraping of metal on metal, car engines. None of it could chase away the darkness pressing down on him. He couldn't open his eyes, couldn't think. At some point, he managed to pry open a heavy eyelid. Fluorescent lights flickered above him, moving—or was he moving somehow? Dizziness rushed him, and he gave into the haze again.

A wave of cold jolted him to sudden consciousness. He jerked back, tried to stand, to run, only to find himself clattering to the ground. Cold metal crashed on top of him. He grunted and flexed his arms. Duct tape bound him to what felt like a folding chair while zipties chafed his wrists. Water dripped from his hair onto a concrete floor. He shivered.

Footsteps drummed against the floor, growing louder. Someone jerked the chair up. It rocked for a moment before Shawn managed to brace his feet against the floor. He stared bleary-eyed into the face of Abounder, now his normal size—or at least what Shawn assumed was the man's normal size. He'd never seen the dude stay the same dimensions for more than a half minute at a time.

Abounder was a beefy fellow even when not expanded, a burly black dude with an impressive beard. He wore a gun-metal gray jumpsuit, probably of some sort of special material that interacted with his powers, since Shawn had never seen it rip during his various transformations. Shawn scanned the room. Above him loomed towering ceilings with exposed wiring and pipes, around him mostly empty space. Maybe some sort of warehouse or garage?

"We have business to discuss," Abounder growled.

"I'm not sure what." Now that Shawn's head had

cleared, an ache rose between his ears. His mouth felt sandpaper dry.

All the disadvantages of a hangover without the blurry memories of a night spent partying. Just what I needed to make this day better.

"You know what!" Abounder gripped Shawn's coat in his fist.

Shawn tried to access his powers, but again they fizzled. At least if he was still wearing the disruptor, DOSA couldn't be far off. They usually installed trackers in those things. Maybe his best bet was stringing Abounder along until rescue arrived.

Man, I hope Crystal and Rapidz are okay.

He focused on Abounder. "My team? Did you hurt them? Or should I say any more of them?"

"As far as I know, they're fine, but don't think that means they'll be coming for you. For one thing, they know as well as I do that you're a traitor. For another, I took the liberty of disabling the tracking device in your disruptor while you were out. They have no way to find us."

Dread settled in Shawn's chest. "I'm not a traitor."

And Abounder should know that. He was working with Maestro. He has to know who the other compromised agent is if there is one. He has to know it isn't me.

"No point in playing dumb for me, kid." Abounder crossed his brawny arms over his chest. "Maestro didn't tell me who on his team was the second man, but he kept hinting that there was one, suggesting he couldn't pull off the heist by himself." He regarded Shawn. "I'm pretty sure he intended to cut you out of the take, though. Is that why you blew him up? Preempting a double cross?"

"You did that!" Shawn stammered.

"Sure." Abounder eyed Shawn. "It's just the two of us here. You don't have to pretend." He reached into a pocket on the side of his suit and drew out a boxcutter.

Shawn tensed. "I'm not playing. You've got the wrong sable."

Abounder clicked up the blade on the boxcutter and started to leisurely trim his nails. "I ain't mad about the whole Maestro thing. Guy made my skin crawl. Not to speak ill of the dead, or whatever."

"Yeah, whatever." Shawn scowled.

"My point is, I don't care that you offed him. If anything you saved me a loose end to tie up. What I do care is that one of you must've stashed the diamond. If you, tell me where it is, and we'll go our separate ways. If him ... well, you better hope you can find it."

"I don't know where it is because I wasn't a part of this at all!" Shawn squirmed in his seat. The duct tape holding him flexed but wouldn't give. He twisted his hands, only to have the zipties about his wrists cut into him. Without his powers, he couldn't get out of this one.

"Are you sure?" Abounder leaned closer, his box cutter's blade glistening in the flickering lights. Shawn's heart jumped into his throat. "There's a lot of pieces of a man that can be removed without killing him, after all." Abounder smiled evilly. "Which are you willing to lose just to keep a diamond? An ear? Fingers? Something more ... essential?"

Shawn flailed for a plan. Could he simply lie his way out of this? Like, if he named a place that Abounder couldn't easily verify, Abounder would have to check it out before he did anything to Shawn.

Right?

If he jumped right into that, it might look suspicious, but he didn't want to lose an ear for the sake of authenticity. Maybe one more try. "Look, you don't need to do this—"

"Nah, but I kind of want to." Abounder winked. "You DOSA types are far too pretty sometimes." He placed the blade against Shawn's thigh, not pressing down hard enough to cut through Shawn's jeans. "Sable healing factor is high, but I've never heard of it regrowing extremities."

"Okay!" Shawn gasped, only half faking his panic.

Abounder drew back.

Shawn took several deep breaths. This needed to be plausible. Somewhere Abounder could get to but that wouldn't be too easy to check. It would've been helpful to know exactly how Maestro had pulled off the heist in the first place. He wasn't even close to the vault when the diamond went missing, and it wouldn't have been easy for him to smuggle it out of the bank—that was it.

"The diamond never actually left the bank," Shawn said.

"Say what?" Abounder frowned.

"Maestro simply moved it from one security box to another, one under his name, so he could get in to get it later." Shawn held eye contact, wanting to appear as trustworthy as possible.

"So how am I supposed to get it, then?" Abounder's jaw clenched. He stabbed into Shawn's thigh.

Shawn inhaled sharply as pain shot up his leg from the cut. Blood seeped through onto his jeans.

Easy, Shawn, that's not deep. You'll be okay. Just keep calm. Don't let him intimidate you. Be smart.

After a moment of self-talk, Shawn gritted his teeth and addressed Abounder again. "He put me on the account as well, but I won't be able to access it unless my name is cleared with DOSA first. You set me free, you find a way to convince DOSA that I'm innocent, and I'll walk in and get it for you. Easy."

Abounder laughed. "And how am I going to do that? If I were that much of a puppeteer with DOSA, I wouldn't need you at all. I'd just have one of their crime scene dudes pick it up for me and send it UPS."

Abounder pulled the blade from Shawn's leg and wiped it on Shawn's coat sleeve before retracting it and shoving the box cutter into his pocket. "So you can't get me the diamond. Tell me why I should keep you alive?"

Shawn's stomach twisted. He'd made his lie too good. Great. Now what?

"Because you're not a murderer." Shawn hoped he didn't sound as uncertain as he felt. "I read your file before the bank heist. You're a thief, definitely a bully, but you don't have any kills on your record. Why start now?"

"On my record being the operative word." Abounder's grin broadened.

"Maybe, but DOSA at least doesn't have knowledge of those kills. If I turn up dead, they'll know it was you—and they'll probably pin Maestro on you too, if I'm not there to take the fall."

"I'm sure they've already got it in their heads that I'm involved with that anyway." Abounder shrugged. "Less embarrassing to blame me than one of their own. If I'm going to go down for something, I'd rather it be something I actually did." He drew his box cutter again.

Images swirled through Shawn's mind, but unlike the cliche, it wasn't his life as he'd lived it so far. Instead, he saw Katie smiling at him in a white dress, a baby with his dark hair and her freckles, himself fighting alongside his father. He wanted that life. He wasn't ready to die.

"Nothing personal kid." Abounder stepped closer.

Shawn kicked out with all his might, both feet going into Abounder's knees. The supervillain stumbled backwards with a cry of pain. Shawn writhed against his bonds. The duct tape twisted but held. Abounder popped up—and up, and up.

Shawn gawped at the now towering supervillain. His adrenaline flared, and his powers responded. They jerked within him like a thousand sparks going off in his blood. He tried to grasp them, to wield them, but they fizzled to a low, desperate hum.

The box cutter, now far too tiny for Abounder's massive hands, clattered to the ground, barely missing

Shawn's foot. Shawn kicked out again, knocking the chair over as Abounder's fist crashed into the floor where he'd been positioned a split second before. The concrete floor cracked beneath the blow.

"I'm going to take you apart with my bare hands!" the villain roared.

"Don't touch him!" a feminine voice shouted.

Shawn rolled, taking the chair with him, to face in the direction of the voice. Crystal stood in the door, eyes on fire.

His heart lightened.

"You going to stop me, lil' girl?" Abounder's voice reverberated through the empty room.

"Not on my own." Crystal snapped her fingers. Three other sables materialized from the shadows, appearing seemingly out of nowhere, two white men in the typical jumpsuits and capes and a bronze skinned woman in a silver jacket and blue leggings. Clouds circled the woman like a halo. Miniature lightning flashed about her. Rain? Katie's team leader? How had she gotten there?

Abounder cursed under his breath before swinging a massive kick at Shawn. The chair absorbed some of the blow's force, but the air still rushed out of Shawn as he spun across the floor. He steadied himself just in time to see Abounder literally crash through a wall.

Crystal rushed to Shawn and knelt beside him. "Are you all right?" she asked, but her voice wasn't Crystal's. A car engine revved in the distance, distracting Shawn from the confusion of Crystal with another woman's voice.

"He's getting away!" He tried to right himself, but the chair made it too awkward.

Crystal's face morphed into Katie's. "Good. If he'd called my bluff a minute ago, we would've been seriously screwed."

Realization crept over Shawn as she cut through the duct tape with Abounder's abandoned box cutter. The remaining three sables—the two dudes he now recognized as other members of Katie's team—stood awkwardly in place, staring at the hole in the wall. Sweat beaded on Katie's forehead.

"None of them are real, are they?" Shawn wriggled free of the remaining tape and angled his body so she could get at the zipties.

"Nope. Do you think Abounder's far enough away that I can let the illusions go?" she asked, her voice strained. The ziptie broke.

"Yeah, I'm pretty sure that was his car peeling out of here." Shawn sat up and rubbed his reddened wrists.

Katie let out a breath, and Rain and the other two illusions puffed out of existence.

"I probably should've used members of your team instead, but I'm not familiar enough with them to be sure I could recreate them convincingly." Katie dabbed at her forehead. "The exception being Crystal, obviously."

Unbound and with the danger passed, Shawn placed his hands on either side of Katie's face and pulled her in for a kiss. She embraced him in return. His heart pounded for a moment before his adrenaline flagged, and his panic calmed.

"You don't know how glad I am to see you again," he breathed into her ear.

"Goes both ways." Her lips fluttered against his, soft, warm, and perfect.

He tried to stand. "We should probably get out of here."

"You're bleeding!" She placed her hand on his leg above the still seeping cut.

"It's not bad. We can worry about it once we're someplace safe." He paused. "I don't know where the nearest safe place is, though."

"Let's get to a drug store or someplace that sells bandages." She stood. "We can patch you up and then figure things out. I passed a few stores on my way here."

He paused as they started towards the hole in the

wall. Beyond stretched a parking lot in what looked like some sort of industrial complex. Various metal buildings, many with truck bay doors, surrounded them.

"Uh, first, how did you find me, and second, how did you get here?" he asked. "You don't even drive."

"First question: check your pocket." She smirked at him.

Already having a suspicion about what he would find, he slipped his hand in and found a cold metal disk. He narrowed his eyes at her. "Okay, admittedly, this time it saved my life, but I have told you that tracking me is kind of a boundary issue, right?"

"Like you said, it saved your life, and it's not like I've been doing it our whole relationship. I just slipped it in there when Crystal came to get you because I had a bad feeling about how that was going to go down. When she called your dad and told him about the attack and how you were kidnapped, it kind of proved me right, though admittedly not in the way I'd expected." She led him into the parking lot. "As for question two: I took an Uber."

"I don't suppose that Uber is still hanging around, waiting for us."

"Nope, so we'd better start walking." She pulled her phone out of her pocket. "Have you ever used Burnr?"

He thought for a moment, examining the tracker with his fingers, before putting it back in his pocket. No point in losing valuable DOSA equipment. "That's that chat app that was in the news a while back? Something about it being banned from schools?"

"Yeah, that's the one." She passed him her now unlocked phone. "It's an untraceable messaging app. Really privacy heavy. Deletes messages after they're sent, can be installed on any device, doesn't log location or collect data."

"I get why schools don't like that. Honestly, I'm surprised the government hasn't tried to kill it yet."

"Oh, they'd like to, and I'd lie if I said it wasn't filled

with terrible people—including most supervillains." She drew a deep breath. "My dad used it for 'networking' but would never let me have it."

"That's probably the only thing you've ever told me about him doing that resembles responsible parenting." Shawn scoffed.

"Well, I have it now. Rain actually hooked the team up on it, said she liked having a way we could contact each other off the record if something went wrong." A slight smile crossed her face. "Rain's cool that way. It's the blue icon that looks like a flame."

He found it. "Okay. I'm assuming you want me to send a message to someone, but I don't know anyone who uses a supervillain chat app."

"You can send an invite to join to a phone number. I think your dad is the best bet. Once he gets it, he can message us, and we can figure out how to meet up." She zipped her coat up to her chin and shivered. "I would've done it, but I didn't know his number off the top of my head."

"Got it." Shawn plugged it into the app. Darkness closed in around them as they left the parking lot for an empty road lit only by occasional streetlamps. "Maybe we should just call DOSA. Tell them where we are and get them to pick us up?"

"Because they've already proven they can do such a good job keeping you safe." He couldn't see her face in the dim light, but from the tone he assumed she was rolling her eyes.

"Yeah, I guess. I at least want to talk to my dad first. Let him know I'm safe again." He glanced at her and his expression softened. "Thanks to you."

Her chin dropped sheepishly towards her chest. "I wasn't going to lose my favorite boyfriend that easily," she then giggled. "Come on. I think I see a gas station up ahead. They'll have a place we can clean up."

Chapter Eleven

Katie fidgeted outside of the men's bathroom. She kept her hoodie up over her head, even though she was pretty sure no one was looking for her—yet.

Shawn emerged from the bathroom. His eyes were tired, and there was a large wet spot on his jeans where it looked like he'd unsuccessfully tried to wash away the blood stain.

"You look like a mess." The words slipped out before she could stop them, and she blushed. "Sorry. That wasn't very nice. You've been through hell tonight."

"It's true, though." He sighed. "I could use some coffee. You want something?"

"I'm good."

He poured himself a cup of black coffee at the drink kiosk before going up to the counter to pay. When he returned to her, he grimaced. "I only have about ten bucks in cash left. If we're going to keep DOSA from tracking me, I probably shouldn't use my debit card."

"What about your phone?" she asked. "They can track that too."

"Rapidz took it before Abounder attacked. Also, Abounder said he disabled the tracking features on this —" He nodded towards his anklet. "So if it hadn't been for your tracker, I would've been off the grid."

She considered his anklet. "It's still suppressing your powers, though?"

"Oh yeah." His face pinched. "It's like walking around half asleep. I feel sluggish and heavy and ... ugh."

"Yeah, I've been there," she said. "I had six months of probation before the SVR would let me be unsupervised without an anklet on. I even slept in one."

"I guess I must sound like a baby whining about it

then." He sipped his coffee.

"I didn't mean that. I was trying to empathize, you know?"

"Yeah, I do." He touched her arm.

Her phone chimed in her pocket. She fished it out. "Your dad got our message."

She opened the chat.

The message read, **Who is this?**

Katie, she typed back. **This chat is secure. I have Shawn. He's okay, but we need to talk to you.**

For a moment the app stayed silent. Then another message popped up. **If Shawn is there, ask him for the passcode.**

Katie's brow furrowed. "Does this make any sense to you?" She showed Shawn the message.

He laughed quietly. "Yeah, it does. It's from back when we were kids. It was a thing for a while to give your kids a 'code' in case a stranger tried to offer them a ride or something, they could verify it was really their parents who had sent them, not a kidnapper. I never actually had a reason to use it. Weird to finally be doing so in my twenties. It's *kimchi*."

She replied with the word.

Where are you?

Katie sent him a map pin to a fastfood place about a block away.

I can be there in twenty minutes. Tell Shawn I'm glad he's safe.

Again, Katie showed Shawn the message.

His posture relaxed. "Maybe it's immature of me, but if he's on his way, I feel like we have a chance."

"I get that." She nodded. Her own experience with her father hadn't been anything she could compare to Shawn's relationship with his, but she'd seen how much the two men meant to each other. Shawn was right. Dave Park would do everything in his power to help his son out of this mess.

Twenty minutes later, the pair sat in the back booth of a burger place, sharing an order of fries that had further depleted Shawn's ten dollar stash. The bell over the door rang, and Dave entered. He made a beeline for their table. Shawn stood to greet him, and his dad pulled him into a bear hug.

"When Crystal called saying Abounder had taken you, I thought I might never see you again." He released his son.

"So Crystal's okay?" Shawn asked. "What about Rapidz and the driver?"

A frustrated smile quirked Katie's lips. Even with everything going on, Shawn was still worried about the team members who had betrayed him.

How very Shawn.

"From what I heard the driver was taken to the hospital with minor injuries but the two sables walked away from the attack." His dad slid into the booth across from Katie. Shawn settled beside her.

The dining area fell silent other than the indistinct noise from the employees taking drive through orders on the other side of the building.

"I don't know what to do, Dad," Shawn began. "My instinct says I need to turn myself in to DOSA, but Katie's worried that they can't keep me safe. She might be right. After all, Abounder snatched me from under Crystal's nose and would've probably killed me if Katie hadn't found me when she did."

Dave concentrated on the tabletop. "Yeah, about that —Shawn, a friend of mine in DOSA's investigatory department—who I won't name because I want you to be able to honestly say you don't know if it ever comes to trial—he emailed me the files on your investigation." He rubbed his forehead as if it hurt. "He was risking his job to do so because it's an ongoing investigation, but he didn't want me blindsided. Things aren't looking good right now."

Shawn's face fell. "I know they found that money in my room, but Maestro must've planted it there. I have no idea how else it could've—"

"It's not just that." His father held up his hand. "Shawn, I love you and I trust you, but this is serious. If you made a mistake, if you got into something over your head, you need to tell me now."

Horror crossed Shawn's face, and Katie's stomach sickened. If Dave Park thought it was possible his son was a criminal, the evidence had to be pretty strong.

"I swear, I haven't done anything wrong—well, not conspiring with supervillains wrong, anyway. I got a speeding ticket a few months ago." Shawn gave an awkward laugh then his expression grew grave again. "I promise, though. I didn't do this. I had nothing to do with Maestro's death or the diamond heist. I love my life. I wouldn't do anything to jeopardize it."

"I thought so, but I needed to hear it from you." Dave let out a breath. "The team traced the serial numbers on the bills you were given. It was plant money. A DOSA undercover agent used it to buy some stolen artwork off Abounder as part of a sting. However, during the exchange, Abounder was bragging about a huge upcoming score, so the agency decided to wait it out and try to catch him at that, rather than go with the lesser 'possession of stolen goods' charge. All the bills found in your room traced back to that drop, and yours were the only fingerprints on the computer."

Shawn sank his face into his hands.

"We already knew that the bills were probably from Abounder, though," Katie put in. "That doesn't mean that Maestro didn't plant them."

"No, but the team has been all over Maestro's finances, and he doesn't show the signs of being in a villain's pocket. All accounts overdrawn. Credit cards maxed. The guy was seriously bleeding red ink." Dave eyed his son. "When was the last time you checked your accounts?"

"Uh—I kind of glance at the notifications I get when my paycheck goes in, but I've got everything set up for automatic payments, so I don't really have a need to— Man, I don't like where this is going." Shawn groaned.

"There was a wire into your account from an offshore one right before the bank heist. It was canceled and re-routed, so the investigators almost missed it, but when my friend told me about it, he described it as a smoking gun."

"This can't be happening." Shawn glanced from his father to Katie and back again. "There's something you need to know, when Abounder had me, he was *very* convinced that I was involved. He thought I had the diamond, that I was the one who killed Maestro. He wouldn't believe me."

"He had to be lying, right?" Katie frowned.

"Whose benefit would he have been lying for?" Shawn held up his hands. "We were the only two people there, and I know I didn't do the things he was accusing me of doing. The thing is, if he didn't kill Maestro, someone else must've, probably someone on my team. That's the only way this makes sense to me. Maestro did have a secret conspirator on the team, one that even Abounder didn't know the identity of. When the bank heist went south, that person must've made off with the diamond thinking he—or she—could leave Maestro to take the fall. Maestro, however, panicked and tried to come clean to me and Rick—so the other conspirator killed him to keep him quiet."

"And now he or she is framing you to tie up the loose ends," Katie breathed.

"It's a complete story that makes sense, but we're missing something kind of important," Dave pointed out. "Proof."

"And also I don't know which team member it is. I don't think it's Crystal." Shawn tapped his fingers thoughtfully on the table top. "She seemed too sincere when she asked me to come clean about it, and if it was her, she wouldn't have tried to warn me like that."

"I hope you're right. We've known each other since the 90s. DOSA may seem like a small world now, but in those early days, there were only a few dozen of us scattered across a half dozen teams around the US. I don't like to think anyone from those days would turn on my son like this, let alone DOSA as a whole." Dave let out a long breath. "So that leaves Pleistocene or Rapidz."

"Maestro seemed to trust Rick—er, Pleistocene," Shawn said. "Honestly, up until this evening, I did too, but he acted strange after the explosion and manipulated me into leaving information out of my testimony ... which I now feel stupid about, but at the time he made it make sense somehow."

"Yeah, that doesn't look good for you. You shouldn't have done that." His father's expression grew stern.

"I know. Believe me, I've kicked myself for that since it happened." The group fell silent again.

Katie squeezed Shawn's uninjured leg beneath the table. With his sable healing factor, the admittedly small cut on his other leg might've healed to the point where she couldn't have hurt him by touching it, but she didn't want to risk it. He slipped his hand on top of hers.

"So what now?" he then asked.

Dave sighed. "We have two options: we trust DOSA to sort this mess out through the legal system, and to keep you safe in the meantime, or we don't."

Katie's chest tightened. "They already let him get kidnapped once, and whoever the other bad guy is, he managed to blow up Maestro and get away clean." She shook her head. "I don't trust them with Shawn right now."

"Unfortunately, neither do I." Dave stood. "Let's get somewhere safe for the night. You both look tired, and I need to make a couple of phone calls. I've given DOSA thirty years. It's time I called in some favors."

Katie leaned against Shawn's shoulder. His dad's arrival hadn't turned out to be the rescue she'd hoped it would be. This wasn't fair. Of all the people she knew, she couldn't think of anyone who deserved this less than Shawn did.

If DOSA won't protect him, I will. Anyone who tries to hurt him has to get through me. I'm not losing him. Not now. Not ever.

Chapter Twelve

When they got into the car, a small sedan Shawn recognized as Juliet's, Dad passed Shawn a yellow file folder. "I printed out everything my friend sent me. Maybe you'll see something I missed in my readthrough. Admittedly, I didn't have a lot of time between getting it and you calling me here."

"Thanks." Shawn opened the file and glanced at the stack of paper within. As his father started to drive, however, his vision blurred, and his head began to nod. He closed his eyes, hoping to rest for a moment.

A slamming car door jerked him awake. They were parked in a mostly empty parking lot outside a cheap looking motel, or MO_EL as the sickly flickering sign read. The driver's seat was empty.

He started as a cool breeze made him realize his door was open.

His father stooped down to look at him. "I've got you a room. Come on. Let's get inside before someone sees us."

He escorted Shawn to room 102. Kate already waited inside, sitting on one of two twin beds with pea soup green bedspreads straight out of the 80s.

"I should've brought you a change of clothes," his father said apologetically.

"I'll be fine. Hopefully this won't last long enough that I'll really need to change." Shawn tried to believe his own words. He had to figure this out. There was too much at stake to just give up.

"Can I see the folder?" Katie asked.

"Sure." Shawn handed it to her. He then sat on the end of the bed and pulled up his pant leg to examine his disruptor anklet. His skin felt raw beneath it, but from what he could see, there was no actual damage, no redness or chafing. Maybe it was all in his head.

Dad's eyebrows shot up. "I'm an idiot. I forgot you were still wearing that. Here." He pulled out his phone and messed with one of his work related apps. The anklet made a whirring sound then fell from Shawn's leg with a pleasing click.

Shawn let out a deep breath as his powers flooded back through him like warmth thawing cold flesh. He drew them out and hovered a foot above the bed for a moment before dropping back onto the mattress with a satisfied sigh. "Good to be whole again."

Dad picked up the disruptor, examined it, and passed it to Shawn. "Keep it. From what I can tell it's still fully functional, and they're handy to have, especially if Abounder comes after you again."

"Thanks, that's smart." Shawn tucked the device, which had coiled into a tight spiral, into his pocket.

Dave shifted from foot to foot. "As much as I want to stay and keep an eye on you, I need to head home to check in with things from the DOSA side. If I try to do that while I'm with you, they might track you down before we're ready."

Katie's muscles tensed. "Can they track your phone? Should you have it on?"

"Yes, they can, but at this point, I think it would look stranger to them if I had it off when they checked in on me. For all they know, Shawn's still being held by Abounder, so me turning my phone off instead of clinging to it hoping for updates will look suspicious. At the same time, though, I can't stay here for too long."

Dad's phone buzzed. He glanced at the readout. "It's my contact with the investigatory team. I need to take this. I'll step outside so you two don't have to stay quiet." He exited the room.

Shawn rubbed his eyes. The short nap in the car hadn't done much for his alertness. He still felt about ready to drift off.

"You should sleep." Katie kissed his cheek.

He shook his head. "Nah, we've got too much work to do. The faster we figure out who is really behind this, and how to prove it, the sooner we can go home." He put his hand in his pocket. Rapidz had taken his phone, but thankfully no one had noticed the small box he also carried. He would've never forgiven himself if Abounder had made off with his mom's precious ring. Now, gazing across the bed at Katie, his plans for proposing during a romantic walk on a crisp December day seemed a distant dream.

Maybe I should just ask her. Forget about the staging and theatrics. Get it out there. Get it set in stone.

He scooted closer to her. "There's something I've been wanting to talk to you about."

"Yes?" She tilted her face towards his, her blue eyes shining in the dim light from the dingy lamps. His breath left him.

"Man, I love you," he whispered.

She fingered his hair. "I love you, too, but it doesn't seem like that's something we need to talk about. It's pretty well established."

"I guess, but sometimes I still have to say it." He eased in for a long kiss.

The door to the room popped open, and he jerked away from her.

"Sorry to interrupt, but I need to talk to you." His father frowned.

"Just me?" Shawn asked.

"It's okay. I want to go over the file." Katie picked the folder off the bed and leafed through its contents.

Heaviness settled over Shawn. Another moment missed. Zipping his coat back up around his chin, he followed his dad outside. They walked a few doors down and stopped on an empty stretch of sidewalk between the hotel and the parking lot. His father kept his eyes on the pavement beneath them.

Shawn's stomach twisted. "What is it?"

"Remember how I said that DOSA still thinks you're Abounder's captive?" his dad asked. "Well ... I was wrong. My contact just told me the official story is now that Abounder's attack was a rescue, breaking an ally out of custody. The assumption is that you are free, on the run, and dangerous."

"Oh." The word came out blandly. Shawn didn't even know what to feel anymore. It was all too much. "What does that mean for us going forward?"

"It means DOSA's actively looking for you. They've put out a bulletin to all agents in the midwest region, but by tomorrow it might go coast to coast." His father avoided Shawn's eyes. "They think you killed one of your own team members and were involved in an attack on two others—this is bad, Shawn. This is really bad."

"Understatement of the year," Shawn mumbled.

So what are my options? DOSA is hunting me. Abounder is hunting me. If I turn myself into DOSA now, maybe it would help my case in the long run, but will they be able to keep me alive in the short term? Especially if they don't even believe there is a real threat from Abounder since they assume we're working together? And that's not even taking into account that one of my team members is apparently a traitor who has already killed once and probably has me in their sights as the next target.

"I was going to call in some favors to get you transferred out of your team's custody into ... any other team, really," his father continued. "With this new information, I don't think I have enough clout for that. I can try, but until you turn yourself in, they won't even listen to my appeals since I can't bargain for a fugitive. However, if you *do* turn yourself in and they still won't agree to it, then you'll be in danger. Your team isn't going to protect you. They've pretty much disowned you for your alleged betrayal."

Shawn stared numbly across the empty parking lot. So that was it? He'd been convicted in absence? Maybe not legally, but for all practical purposes DOSA had condemned him for something he hadn't done. His hand strayed to his pocket, clutching the ring box inside as if it were his last link to the life he'd felt so certain of only a few days before.

A lump formed in his throat.

I can't drag Katie into this. It's not fair. She's worked so hard to escape the villain life. Maybe I'm not a villain, but with how this is going, I'm definitely an outlaw.

Hardening his determination, he pulled the box out of his pocket and held it out to his father. Dave Park blinked at it.

Shawn let out a breath. "I can't accept this. I don't know where I'll be from now on, if I'll have a chance to use it. If something happened to it—I can't be the reason Mom doesn't get a chance to start her family tradition." He pushed it at his father who kept his hands at his sides.

"Shawn," Dave's voice came out in a rasp. "You can't give up—"

"How can I not?" Shawn's resistance broke, his words turning into a wail. "I've lost everything, Dad. My career, my future, and if I don't keep moving, my freedom if not my life." He closed his eyes. "I keep trying to find a way out, a way back, to fix this, but if what you're saying is true, there might not be one. I can't prove I didn't do this. Abounder wants me dead. DOSA wants me in disruptor cuffs. I've got people coming at me from both the villain and the hero sides." He sank onto the curb, head in his hands. "I have never felt so helpless—so alone."

Dave settled next to him. His hand gripped his son's shoulder. "You're not alone. I am not going to let you be alone."

Shawn laughed bitterly. "So you're going to go on the run with me?"

"If that's what—"

"Stop," Shawn interrupted. "You're not."

"You're my son," Dave's voice sharpened. "I can't abandon you."

"And Mom? Abigail and Jules? Can you abandon them?"

The fire faded from his father's eyes.

"Because that's the choice you'd have to make. It's not like the whole family can disappear with me. Heck, Abs and Mom don't even have superpowers. They aren't cut out for this." Shawn massaged his forehead. "Remember what Mom said when I told her about ... about Katie?" He couldn't bring himself to be more specific. The details of that talk were too painful with everything that he'd lost.

"Something to the extent of you being all grown up now, if I remember correctly," Dave murmured.

"And I guess she was right. This is my mess. Whether I asked for it or not, I have to face it. I'm not going to drag you or the rest of the family or ... Katie—" he forced her name out with some effort, "—into danger because I can't handle myself. That wouldn't be being a man, would it?"

"I suppose not." Dave's hold on Shawn tightened until it hurt, but Shawn leaned into it. All his life, he'd wanted to be like his father, to live up to that legacy, to prove that he was worthy of the love and support he'd been given so unconditionally. That was gone now. He'd lost his chance. The best he could hope for now was simply not to hurt him any further. His vision blurred.

"I ... If I never see you again, though, Dad—it's gonna break my heart."

Dave tackled Shawn in a hug.

Father and son held each other for a long moment before Shawn pulled away. He held up the ring box again, doing his best to keep his expression firm.

Dave sighed, took it, and tucked it into his pocket.

"Not forever. It's still yours, and I still want to see it on Katie's finger in the near future, but for now, I'll hold onto it. For safekeeping until we get this worked out."

"Safekeeping. Sure." Shawn nodded.

Dave scanned the parking lot. "If I keep working on this from within DOSA, I might be able to figure out what happened with your team. I trust Crystal. She's wrong about you, but she's been loyal to DOSA for almost as long as I've been with the department. I can't see her risking an over twenty year career to join forces with a mid-range villain like Abounder. That said, your team has to have a mole. It's the only explanation."

"With Maestro dead that leaves Rapidz and Rick—er —Pleistocene." Shawn chewed on his bottom lip. "I hate to say this because I actually like Rick, but he's the more likely. It was weird how he acted after the explosion."

"I'll keep an eye on him, then." Dave stood and glanced back in the direction of the hotel. "So that's me. What about Katie?"

Shawn's heart twisted. "She needs to go back with you."

"Is she going to want to, though?" Dave asked.

"I'll have to convince her." Shawn stood. "Can you give me five minutes?

"Take all the time you need."

Feeling like he was walking to his own execution, Shawn returned to their hotel room. When he entered, he found Katie standing over one of the beds, the contents of the file spread out in front of her.

"Hey, where's your dad?" she asked in a surprisingly enthusiastic voice.

"Still outside." He peered over her shoulder. "What are you doing?"

"I was going over the details of the bank heist, and I found something." She passed him a piece of paper detailing the bank's security systems. In the center of the first paragraph, one word had been underlined,

"DeField."

Shawn scanned the text around it. "So the camera system was made by DeField Industries—" He tilted his head to one side. "Should that mean something to me?"

"It means something to me!" she said excitedly. "I'm familiar with that system. According to the bank it was installed almost four years ago."

"So it's out of date?" He tried to keep up.

"No, not really. They patch these things, and most banks can't afford to replace their full system every couple of years. It's just not practical, plus installing a new system and working out the bugs leaves the bank open to short term breaches—it's complicated, but that's not my point." She inhaled a deep breath. "It means that this sort of system was in use when I was still a villain. I'm familiar with it. I know how it works, and the security guard was right: the files couldn't be deleted from the system remotely. It's an intentionally isolated system. All self-contained."

Shawn nodded slowly. "So you're saying it had to be done by someone in the bank?"

"Exactly. So that means Abounder, the security guard, or one of your team. Are we thinking one of your team? From this report, I don't think Abounder had the time to do it. To make sure all the backup files were deleted, he would've needed several minutes, and your team clocked him pretty quickly after he got to the bank."

"Yeah, also someone besides him got into the vault and cleared out the box. He wouldn't be coming after me if he had the diamond already." Shawn tapped his fingers against his leg. This wasn't what he needed to talk to her about, but if she'd found something he could use to help his case, he wanted to know. Also—he really didn't want to tell her what he was supposed to tell her. "The problem is, I don't know if any one member of my team was ever in a place to do that. Maestro never even entered the building. Rapidz and Crystal stayed together, and Rick and I spent the whole heist in sight of each other."

"So you think it was the guard?" She picked up a small stack of papers. This one had a black and white picture of the security guard on the first page. "His personal records seem pretty tame. Like, don't get me wrong, I know from experience that pressure or bribery can get a long standing company man with a good record to do all sorts of things their work history paints as unlikely, but I'm sure DOSA has looked into this guy. If he'd taken a bribe or was being blackmailed, wouldn't they know it?"

"Maybe." Shawn rubbed the back of his neck. His recent experiences had shaken his confidence in DOSA's investigation process.

"I think we should talk to him, though. Like I said, I have inside knowledge on how villains get to people like this guard. I might be able to break him if I can just ask the right questions." She started to pick up the papers and put them back in the folder. "So that's our next step, right? We go talk to the guard and see if Abounder paid him off?" She gazed up at him, her beloved blue eyes so sincere.

Get it over with, Shawn. Rip off the Band-Aid. It's not going to get any easier.

"Katie, we need to talk." He sat on the edge of the bed.

Her bottom lip quivered. "Is something wrong? Well, I guess a lot of things are wrong, but something else? Something new?"

"Not exactly." His whole being ached to pull her onto his lap and hold on for dear life, but he couldn't think about what he wanted right now. He had to think about what was best for her. "My dad is going home to see if he can keep working on this from inside DOSA."

"That seems smart." She nodded. "He has influence, and it's good to know we have someone in the department who's still on our side."

"I want you to go with him." He forced his gaze to meet hers.

She stared at him, her face blank. "That doesn't make any sense."

That hadn't been the reaction he'd expected. "Yeah, it does."

"No, it doesn't," she repeated. "Shawn, your dad has contacts in DOSA. I don't. If I go back, the only thing I'll be able to do is sit on my hands and wait, and I don't want to do that. I don't like that."

"But you'll be safe," he protested.

"But you won't." She crossed her arms over her chest.

Shawn wanted to say he was okay with not being safe if it meant she was, but he had a hunch that wouldn't go over very well. Instead he tried another tack. "Look, if DOSA catches you with me, you'll lose your SVR deal. You've worked so hard to become a hero—"

"So we don't let them catch us." She sat beside him. "Shawn, you can't do this on your own. I'm sorry, but as good a hero as you are, we're in my world now. I know more about how to work on this side of the law than you do. This isn't going to last long. I know we'll find a way to prove you're innocent in no time, but if you want to survive long enough to reach that point, you need me."

He shook his head. "I can't see you get hurt because of me. I won't do anything stupid. I promise. I'll lie low—"

"Shawn, do you know how to get a hotel room without a valid ID?" She frowned at him.

"Uh... I mean, we've got this one." Had his dad used an ID? He hadn't thought to ask.

"You can't stay in one place for too long. Not with people looking for you, which brings up another point. What about if you need transportation? Let's say you want to flee the state. Have you ever hotwired a car?" She narrowed her eyes at him.

"I would rather not do that. I'm already in enough trouble—"

"But if it's a choice between stealing a car and letting Abounder catch up with you? Are you really going to die because you aren't willing to steal?"

His stomach twisted. "If those are the only two choices—but there has to be another way. Bus tickets, maybe?"

"Requires ID—but maybe you want to get a fake one of those. I'm sure you know people who can make them, right?"

"Yeah—" He searched for a point in his favor. "I can fly."

"Oh, that's not conspicuous at all." She clicked her tongue.

They sat in silence for a long moment. Shawn's thoughts churned. If he really needed her, if she could really help him, maybe he should let her stay. After all, they had a better chance of surviving together, and if he had to leave everyone else he loved behind, it would be nice to have this one person, his best person, to hold onto.

I've lost everything, but if I can keep her in my life, then it won't be so bad—but what sort of life would I even be offering her? No, I can't be selfish here. I can't—

Her hand brushed across his shoulders. "Shawn," she whispered.

He looked into her eyes, and his heart broke open. "I love you, Katie. I can't ask you to put yourself in danger for me—"

"You put yourself in danger for me." She took his hand. "A little over a year ago a young supervillain who had been brainwashed into thinking she had nothing good to offer the world took a chance by putting her faith in a kind young superhero. My life was hellish before you came into it. I wasn't my best self, and I knew it, but worse than that, I didn't have anyone who thought I could be more. You plucked me out of that cage and taught me that I can be a hero." Her hold about his fingers tightened. "I owe you. Even if I wasn't head over heels, stupid in love with you, I'd want to pay you back for what you did for me." She kissed his cheek. "Let me pay my debt. Let me help you like you helped me."

Unable to resist any longer, he drew her into an embrace. She slipped easily onto his lap, like she belonged there, a perfect fit where nothing could come between them. Her lips met his, and he melted into her. Her hands gripped his shirt as his disappeared into her soft red hair. They parted for a breath.

"I don't want you to lose everything," he breathed. *The way I might already have.*

"If we're smart, I won't." She brushed her hand up into his hair. "My team isn't expecting me back for over a week. What I do in my off time isn't their business, and I can use illusions to make sure no one sees us together." Her face shifted, her hair fading to a pale yellow, her nose straightening and growing a little longer. Her eyes strobed from blue to green a few times before settling on a mix between the two colors. "What do you think?"

"I like the real you better, but yeah, this is probably smart." He brushed his hand across her cheek, and she reverted to her true appearance. "I guess I should tell my dad that the plan's changed again."

He stepped out of the room to find his father waiting, a grin on his face.

"She's staying with you, isn't she?" Dave asked.

"Uh, yeah." Shawn gave a sheepish smile. "I kind of lost that argument."

"I'm not going to lie and say I'm mad about that." Dave clasped his son's arm. "I'll feel better knowing she's with you. Be careful, though, Shawn." He passed him a cell phone. "This is a burner. Bought with cash, pay as you go. Even so, only use it if you really need to."

"Thanks." Shawn tucked the phone into his pocket. "I'll download the Burnr app, in case we need to contact you."

"Good idea. Also, take this." His dad passed him an envelope.

Peeking inside, Shawn found a stack of fifty dollar bills. He balked. "I can't—"

"You can pay me back later, but you can't risk using your cards right now. Knowing you, I very much doubt you have more than a few dollars in cash on you." His father gave him a knowing look.

Pushing down his pride, Shawn pocketed the money. "Thanks. I will pay you back for what I use. I promise."

"I also want to leave you the car. It's registered to Juliet, her graduation present, so I think it will fly under DOSA's radar when they put out their bulletins." His dad held out the keys.

"Is she going to be okay with that?" Shawn frowned.

"I told her she could use your truck until I brought it back, and she told me to tell you if you damaged her vehicle in any way, she'd lay claim to yours in perpetuity."

"That's fair."

His dad pulled him into a quick hug. "Be careful, Shawn."

"I will. Tell Mom and the girls I love them and I'm okay. We'll get through this." Shawn closed his eyes, willing himself to believe it.

Unable to watch his father leave, he slipped back into the room. Katie wasn't there, but he could hear the shower running in the bathroom. He kicked off his shoes and settled onto one of the beds. His whole being felt tired, but he didn't know if he'd be able to sleep. He could've used a change of clothes or at the very least a toothbrush. Determined to try to rest, he turned off the light and rolled over onto his side.

His mind wandered to Katie. They'd be spending the night in the same room. No house rules here.

What if I can't fix this, though? If everything goes back to normal again, then that's one thing, but if it doesn't? No, this isn't the time to make choices like that. Fix my life, then enjoy it.

Determination steeled, he closed his eyes. The bathroom door opened, and her footsteps padded across the thin carpet.

"Shawn, are you awake?" she whispered.

"Yeah, mostly," he replied. "Tired though."

"Me too but ... I don't want to be alone tonight. Can we sleep together?"

He propped himself up on his elbows. "Do you mean sleep or ... sleep?"

"Just real sleep." She sat on the edge of the bed. "I'm tired too and ... I'm a little worried about what's happened on these sheets." She wrinkled her nose, vaguely visible in the dim light seeping from around the curtains.

He laughed quietly. "Best not to think about that." He scooted a little closer to the opposite edge of the bed. "I think I'll fall asleep easier with you to hold onto."

"Good." She lay next to him and rested her head on his chest. His arms surrounded her. The warmth and weight of her soothed his soul. Listening to the quiet calm of her breathing, Shawn drifted off to sleep.

Chapter Thirteen

Katie fidgeted in her seat as they turned onto a residential road lined with narrow brick homes, most similar in layout with very little space between them. Not nearly as nice as Shawn's family's house, but still better than any of the hotels she'd grown up in. Her legs were cramping from the long drive from Ohio to St. Louis.

"I hope he's home after we came all this way," she said.

"Considering that his bank was robbed out from under him just a few days ago, I'm guessing he's on leave. If he's not there, we'll wait. Not like I have anywhere else to be." Shawn glanced at the GPS. "It's the house right up here."

They pulled to a stop in front of a house much like the others, but this one with gray stone planters on the porch, filled with dead tomato plants with a few shriveled tomatoes still clinging desperately to the vines. Shawn turned off the engine and reached for the door handle.

"Wait!" Katie grabbed him by the arm. She focused on his face, extending her powers as if she were painting a picture over his features. Her powers trickled down his body, changing his long sleeved t-shirt and stained jeans into a sharp black suit and plain tie. "There. Take a look." She nodded towards the rear-view mirror.

Shawn arched his now gray eyebrow, glanced at the mirror, and recoiled at the face of the middle-aged white guy looking back at him.

"What the—" He touched his face. "Man, that's freaky."

"Let me do a quick adjustment to myself." She put on her blond persona and changed from her casual clothes to a suit identical to his, only tailored to the female form.

"How's this?" she asked.

"Nice. So we're impersonating DOSA agents now? That's got to be illegal." He sighed.

"Technically we're both DOSA agents. We just don't want anyone to know which agents we are." She allowed herself a smirk. "Let's go."

They climbed up the steps to the porch, and Shawn rapped lightly on the door. After a few minutes, a man of about forty wearing sweatpants and a worn Pink Floyd t-shirt opened the door and scrutinized them.

"Hank Aragon?" Shawn asked.

"Yeah, that's me." Hank cast a wary glance over both of them. "Are you with DOSA?"

"Yes," Katie said eagerly. "I'm Agent Rembrant and this is Agent Van Gogh."

Shawn gave her a sideways glance that very clearly said, "Seriously?"

She ignored him. If she was going to have a secret identity, she wanted it to be cool. "We'd like to know if we can come in and ask you a few questions about the recent incident," she continued.

"Can I see some ID?" Hank drew back, pulling the door half shut with him.

"Certainly." Katie reached into her pocket and imagined an ID card forming. It took shape, growing solid in her grasp. Hopefully she'd seen enough DOSA IDs for this one to pass muster. She pulled it out and held it forth.

Hank squinted at it. "Yeah, I guess that looks good. Come on in. Sorry about the mess. I've been kind of slumming it since I got put on leave."

Katie held the card illusion until he turned away then let it poof out of existence. Under her projected mask, her expression tightened. Holding multiple illusions active at the same time had always been hard, though she'd gained some stamina over the last year or so.

Hank led them into a living room cluttered with pizza

boxes and other take out containers. A muted TV played commercials, but Hank turned it off before sitting in a worn recliner. He motioned towards the couch.

"I don't know what more I can tell you. I went over everything with DOSA, the police, and the bank's management." He dropped his gaze to his lap. "I hate to have this loss on my record, after so many years working security, but I'm just a normal guy. What am I going to do against supervillains?"

"Nothing, and DOSA wouldn't expect you to put yourself in harm's way against one." Shawn smiled sympathetically, his fake wrinkles deepening with the gesture. "That's our job, not yours."

Doing her best to keep it inconspicuous, Katie examined their surroundings. A nice-ish TV, more standard than huge, furniture that looked to be a few years old, food from basic restaurants—this guy wasn't living like someone who had come into money. That didn't mean he wasn't in need of it, though.

"Does your job pay well, Mr. Aragorn?" she asked.

"Uh, it's Ara-gon. Like the place in Spain, not like the dude from those movies."

"Sorry."

"No problem. I get that a lot," he said. "As for the job, it's not great money, but it's just me here. I inherited this house from my mom, so I own it outright. I make enough to pay the bills, put a little into retirement, and have some left over to attend a couple concerts or maybe a Rams game now and then." He gave an awkward chuckle. "Also, there aren't a lot of jobs where if nothing happens, it's a good day. I like it. I really feel rotten that it went wrong, but what could I do ... like ... I hope I don't get fired over this."

"I'm sure you won't. Like you said there wasn't anything you could've done to stop it," Shawn assured him.

"I hope you're right." Hank's face took on a glum

expression.

Something within Katie itched. She knew a little about lying. She didn't think Hank was lying outright, but he was leaving something out, something that made him anxious about losing his job.

"Do you have any idea how the security tapes could've been wiped?" she asked.

"No, not really. I followed procedure. As soon as the police secured the area, I tried to back up the recordings, but they were already gone."

"Do you have any idea when that would've happened?" she pushed.

"Uh, not really." His eyes darted from side to side.

Katie leaned forward in her seat. "How about you give me a timeline from when you got in to work that night to when you pulled the tapes?"

"Okay, sure, I guess. I clocked in and did the checklist. It's the same every night—" He swallowed. "I need some water. Is that all right?"

"Of course." Shawn nodded.

They both watched Hank walk out of the room towards the kitchen.

Shawn kept his eyes on the door. "Do you think he's going to run?" he whispered. "He's hiding something."

"Yeah, but I don't think it's a criminal conspiracy." Katie's gaze swept the room. "I saw Dad bribe his fair share of security guards, and they fall into two camps: there's the cold, calculating type who are fine lying to their employer's face and don't buckle under pressure, but you can also get the amateurs who can't handle it and break down sweating bullets at the first sign of interrogation. This dude's weirdly in the middle. He's anxious but not in a 'my life is ruined and I am going to go to jail' way. More in a 'I hope I don't lose my pretty basic job' way." She bit her bottom lip. "I'm going to try something. It's a risk, but I have a feeling it might work."

"Go for it." Shawn nodded.

Katie rose, let her illusion slip, and walked into the kitchen. Hank stood at the sink, rinsing out a water glass.

"Who are you and where did you come from?" he stammered.

"I'm this." She let her illusion re-form for a split second before it faded again. The glass hit the bottom of the sink and shattered.

Hank gaped at her. "That's freaky."

"So in case it wasn't too obvious, I'm not a DOSA agent," she said.

"Uh, then what *are* you?"

"I'm someone who needs to know what happened the night of the robbery but is under no obligation to tattle to your bosses about it." She held his gaze. "Look, Hank, I don't think you're a criminal. I think you're an honest guy who is worried about losing his job because of something that isn't even his fault."

Hank's mouth twisted as if he'd tasted something bitter. "It might actually be my fault."

"Either way, I'm not here to report on it. I just need to know what happened. We're not after you. We're trying to figure out who took the diamond, and I'm willing to bet money that it wasn't you."

His eyes widened. "People think I took the diamond?"

"No. I don't. As far as I know DOSA doesn't either," she soothed. "Someone did, though, and what happened that night might be the key to figuring out who."

"Yeah, I doubt that," Hank mumbled.

Shawn joined them from the kitchen. Her attention had lapsed during her conversation with Hank, and Shawn's appearance had returned to normal. Hank cast him a confused glance before continuing.

"I have worked that job for almost two decades, since right out of high school, and I've never fallen asleep on the clock. *Never.* I wasn't even tired. I had a good nap the afternoon before my shift. I shouldn't have fallen asleep. I just ... I did." He hung his head. "I had just finished walking the floor, so I sat down for a minute to watch the security cameras. I do that between rounds. Anyway, I was sitting there, watching, then ... everything went fuzzy then black, almost like I passed out but without any reason. When I woke up, the alarms were going off and there were super people duking it out in the lobby. It was a mess." He cringed. "I not only fell asleep at my post, I somehow slept right through a robbery. If my bosses find out—"

"They won't," Katie promised.

Dang it. That wasn't what I hoped. This doesn't help at all.

She glanced at Shawn expecting to find him equally disappointed. Instead, his eyes were alight and intense.

"That means something to you?" she asked.

"It means Maestro wiped the tapes. A blackout like that is exactly what someone would experience if he jumped into their body and puppeted them for a short while. Loss of perception followed by loss of time."

Hank's hands shook. "You mean a villain took over my body? Like a horror movie or something? Like an alien parasite?" He cringed and scratched at the back of his neck as if he could feel chest bursters crawling beneath his skin.

"Not exactly, but close enough. Don't worry. You're safe now. The guy's dead." Shawn grunted in irritation. "Look, don't tell DOSA we were here, but come clean about the blackout. It won't get you in the trouble you think, and it'll help with their investigation, all right?"

"Yes, sir." Hank nodded frantically. "Can they make sure he's not still in my brain, though? Is there a way to be sure?"

"Like I said, he's dead. You're safe." Shawn motioned to Katie. "Let's get out of here."

Katie hurriedly followed Shawn from the kitchen. She had just enough time to throw up a quick illusion disguise over them both before he stormed out of the house, slamming the door behind them.

She watched in confusion and distress as he settled into the driver's seat of his sister's car and sank his head against the steering wheel.

Slipping into the passenger seat, she reached across and touched his wrist. "Are you all right?"

"No." His chest rose and fell in a great breath. "We already knew Maestro was dirty. What Aragon told us confirms that. It also suggests that Maestro was working alone. Except we know he wasn't because someone killed him." He looked up at her. "Don't you think it's weird that Abounder and Maestro were both working with this individual but neither of them knew the guy's identity? How were they communicating with them? I'd say Maestro lied to both us and Abounder about having a co-conspirator at all except then we're left with Maestro blowing himself up, which makes no sense."

An idea struck Katie. "Are we sure Maestro is dead, then? What if he faked his own death so he could escape with the diamond and leave you and Abounder to take the fall?"

"Only if he was able to clone himself and somehow swap places with his clone last minute. The body in the car was decently toasted, but dental records and DNA both confirmed it was him. That would be hard to fake even assuming that Maestro somehow hid a secondary teleporting ability from the team and was able to zap himself away and some other poor dude into the car in the split second before it exploded." He hid his face in his hands. "I'm stuck, Katie. I don't know where to look next or what to do."

She massaged his arm. "Hey, I get it. This isn't what we wanted to hear, but we're no worse off than we were. Let's get some place quiet and go over the files again. Maybe get a message to your dad and see what he's come up with, okay?"

"I guess." The despair in Shawn's voice twisted her heart.

She kissed his cheek. "We'll get through this, Shawn. I know we will, and if we don't ... well, there are worse people to start a new life with."

Though she'd meant that to be encouraging, Shawn's face contorted further, and he looked away from her. "Let's get going. I need to think."

Chapter Fourteen

Shawn considered staying in St. Louis to continue the investigation, but with no way to access the bank and all the major players still in Columbus, he decided to return to Ohio again. If he were honest with himself, he just wanted to be nearer to his family.

Katie suggested changing motels to keep pursuit off their trail. Before they settled in for the night, they stopped at a store and picked up some toiletries and a change of clothes. Even with Katie's projection hiding his true appearance, Shawn couldn't help but squirm as he interacted with the cashier. He instinctively ducked his head when he walked past other customers.

Their new motel was hardly an improvement from the previous one. A faint smell of cigarette smoke lingered in the furnishings, and his skin itched just looking at the drab, mustard yellow bedspread. His shoulders slumped.

Maybe I can start a new life, but will it be a life I even want to live?

Katie put her hand on his arm. "Why don't you take a shower? I bet it will make you feel better."

"Worth a shot." He picked up his change of clothes and a bottle of body wash and entered the bathroom. "It's not like I could feel any worse." He gazed sullenly into the cracked mirror above the sink.

Closing his eyes against the mildew and years of soap scum, he stepped under the hot water and savored the feel of it running down his face and over his chest. He exhaled.

Come on, Shawn, you always do your best thinking in the shower. There has to be a way out of this.

What did he need? He needed a way to prove he didn't do this, but proving a negative was hard. His one attempt to discover who had done it had come to a dead end. He'd gone over the file multiple times. If there was a clue in there, he would've found it.

It's got to be Rick. Dang, though, I would've sworn he was sincere when he was scolding Maestro for betraying the team, so he's either a great actor or a massive hypocrite—or I'm not as good a judge of people as I thought I was.

The diamond had to be the key. It was what Abounder wanted, what had tempted two DOSA heroes to turn aside from everything they claimed to stand for.

If I can recover it, that might work as a point in my favor, plus once DOSA has it, Abounder won't be after me anymore ... but where is it?

He sudsed up his hair before stepping back under the stream of water to rinse. That done, he turned off the water and reached for one of the towels folded on the bathroom counter.

We know for sure it was in the security deposit box when the bank closed for the evening. Abounder could get into the vault, but not get out with the diamond because his powers don't transfer to objects. Even if he squeezed himself under the door, he wouldn't be able to take the diamond with him. That lie I made up for Abounder, about just moving it to another box, is actually the perfect method, assuming he had someone who could go back in for it later, maybe whoever owned the second box. However, Abounder doesn't know where it is, so Maestro would've had to do it. Maybe he puppeted someone to move it for him. Of course, Maestro claimed he didn't know where the diamond was. Maybe he was lying?

He finished toweling off and quickly dressed.

Katie sat on the end of the bed, legs crossed. "I ordered pizza. It should be here soon."

"Great." He forced a smile.

She stood and brushed her hand across his cheek.

"Feeling any better?"

"Good enough. Just glad to be with you." He kissed her forehead.

"I'm going to try and get a shower in before the pizza gets here." She picked up the shopping bag that contained her half of their earlier purchases. "Why don't you see if there's anything good on TV? I think we both need a break. Maybe a movie to watch."

"In a minute. I'm going to text my dad and let him know we're still okay." He picked up his phone from the nightstand and pulled up the Burnr app as she disappeared into the bathroom.

A new notification popped up.

Contact request? From who?

He clicked on it and read: **Shawn, this is Rain, Katie's team leader. I need to talk to you.**

The hair on the back of his neck prickled. Could this be a trap?

He tapped out, **How'd you get my contact information?**

Your dad. We talked on the phone today. I had to promise I didn't want to do you harm, and he told me to tell you 'kimchi' whatever that means.

Shawn's tension eased somewhat. **What do you want?**

First off, don't tell me if Katie is with you or not. I would rather not know. I know from the way she talks about you that she trusts you with her life. She's technically on leave right now, but she's still with the SVR, and she missed her last check-in call.

Shawn winced. Katie had made it sound as if Rain wouldn't come looking for her yet. Of course it couldn't be that easy.

Your dad seems to think you're innocent, and I know Katie probably does as well, Rain continued. **Look, Shawn, I want to believe that you mean**

125

well for Katie, but if she doesn't check-in soon, I'll have to report it to my superiors. Once I do that, consequences start kicking in for her.

His stomach twisted. **What sort of consequences?**

Short term: loss of the freedoms she's earned over the last few months, returning to her wearing a disruptor cuff, phone and computer privileges revoked. Long term—and this is purely hypothetical. I'm not saying this is happening at all. For all I know she's just sitting in her guest room at your dad's house and has simply forgotten to call in. That said, if DOSA found out that she were, for instance, on the run with someone who is currently wanted by the department, it could cost her her deal. She might end up in a holding cell with no foreseeable chance of reentering the SVR. The system is not friendly to those perceived as backsliding.

Shawn rested his forehead in his hand, drew a deep breath, then typed. **How long does she have?**

She needs to check in by midnight or I'll be forced to issue my report. If that report reaches HQ, there will be a team sent to verify her location.

Shawn glanced at the digital clock on the bedside table. 8 p.m. ... It was an hour earlier in Wichita, so maybe they had a little more time, but not much.

I don't want to cost her anything. I swear, I didn't do this, but I can't prove it. He closed his eyes. If he could prove his innocence, that was one thing, but so far he'd failed, and Katie's time was running out. He couldn't be selfish here. It was time for her to go home.

Desperate not to say goodbye, he switched chats to send a message to his father. Maybe Dad could provide him with some hope. **Any good news?**

After a moment his father replied. **I'm afraid not. Rain called from the Wichita branch looking for Katie. I didn't tell her anything, but I gave her your contact information.**

I know. He closed his eyes. Katie would not lose her freedom because of him. Before he could talk himself out of it, he typed again. **You need to come get her. We're in room 210 here.**

He attached a link.

I won't be here when you arrive. I love you, Dad. Can you make sure she's safe for me?

I'll leave now. Hang in there, Shawn. I'm not giving up.

Unable to think of more to say, Shawn placed his phone in his pocket and started to gather up his belongings. He'd just finished stuffing them all into a cheap backpack he'd picked up during their shopping trip when the water turned off in the bathroom. Shawn's heart jumped into his throat. As cowardly as it might've been, part of him had wanted to disappear before she emerged. He didn't trust that she wouldn't talk him out of leaving again.

No, even if I could do that, it wouldn't be right. She needs to understand even if she doesn't agree.

She emerged, dressed in leggings and a sweatshirt, her long red hair still wrapped in a towel. "No pizza yet?"

"No." He shook his head. "Katie, Rain got in touch with me through the Burnr app."

She stiffened. "It's because I missed a check-in, isn't it? I was trying to figure out a way to do it without them tracking my location." She glanced at the clock. "I still have time. Rain lets me be a few hours late. Hopefully if I check-in she won't feel a need to verify my location. She doesn't have a reason to think I'm with you."

"Yeah, she does." Shawn's chest tightened. "She didn't come out and say she knew, but she hinted around it enough."

Katie swallowed. "That's not good."

"No, it's not." He closed his eyes. "Katie, I asked my dad to come get you."

She stared at him for a moment, her lower lip trembling, then her face hardened. "No."

"Yes!" Frustration and grief welled up within him. He wanted to touch her, to hold her, to kiss her and pretend this wasn't happening—but he couldn't. "You've worked so hard to get where you are right now. If you don't go back with him, you're going to lose that. Lose everything—"

"I owe all that to you, though—" She took a step towards him, but he pulled away, heart pounding.

"No, you don't." He steadied himself again. "You tell yourself that, but you made the choice to step away from your father, to help me when he tried to harm me rather than go along with it. Also, I introduced you to the SVR, but I didn't invent them. You owe me absolutely nothing."

"That's not true." She shook her head, her eyes reverting to the sad, hurt child look that had first drawn him to her, a shy girl in a coffee shop who needed him to cheer her up. Seeing her grow out of that sadness, embracing her sparkle as she found her freedom with the SVR, it had been everything to him. He couldn't cost her that, even if in the moment it hurt like nothing he'd ever felt before. Even so, he couldn't look into her eyes as he continued.

"It is. You're not some victim any more. You've made your own choices for a long while, but if you stay with me, you'll lose that. You'll be a fugitive again, and if DOSA catches us, you'll be a prisoner—"

"That's my choice, though," her tone grew firmer. "I'll take that chance to be with you."

"I can't let you do that." He struggled to remember what Rain had said, how it would cost Katie if he didn't do what he needed to do.

"It's not just you making the decision." She caught his hand. "We love each other. We ... we're better together. We're ... we're a couple. We're us."

"Maybe right now it's best if we aren't that." The words tasted bitter on his tongue. Her hold on his hand loosened.

"What do ... what?"

His own determination choked him. "For the time being, we're not an us. We're not anything because I've lost everything, and I'm not going to drag you down with me. You're free. You have your life, and I have ... I have one last chance to fix this, but I can't do it at a cost to you." He released her hand and took a step back, shouldering his backpack.

"Shawn, don't say that. Don't ..." Her voice cracked. "Don't do this."

"I'm sorry, Katie." He opened the door and stepped out onto the second story walkway. A few feet away, stairs led down to the first level. He had no intention of going down, though.

"Shawn—" she began, her voice taking on a warning tone.

Shawn spun around, accessed his powers, and jumped over the railing. The darkness of the night cloaked him as he pushed himself through the cold winter air, refusing to look back.

Chapter Fifteen

Shawn got about two blocks from the motel before he realized he'd forgotten to take the car. He doubled back for it, staying near the edge of the parking lot until he was sure Katie wasn't watching before fishing the keys out of his pocket and hurrying to claim it. He debated hanging around until his dad got there, but that would both give Katie more opportunity to find and confront him and lead to another goodbye with his father—neither of which he was sure he could handle right now. Instead, feeling raw, he drove into the night.

After about a half hour of driving in no particular direction, his stomach growled. Without Katie's illusions to protect him, he didn't feel safe going into a restaurant. Thank goodness for drive throughs. He found one he liked, purchased his food, and parked at the far end of the parking lot to eat in dark and silence.

I'm really on my own this time.

He took a sip of his soft drink and stared out the window into the darkness.

Maybe I should go back to St. Louis, try to see if I can get in touch with people who know the villain scene. Whoever took the stone, they'll have to sell it eventually. They'll need contacts for that. It's a long shot, but worth a try.

He probably couldn't make St. Louis tonight, but he could at least drive a few hours before he'd need to pull over and rest. Plus he'd be safer outside of Columbus where DOSA was actively looking for him.

Course decided, he popped the last few fries into his mouth, collected all his garbage into the paperbag his order had come in, and turned the key.

A low fuel warning flashed on the dash.

Crap.

He could see a gas station sign just down the road, so that wasn't a problem, but to get fuel with cash, he'd have to go into the building. There'd be cameras and he didn't have Katie to disguise him anymore.

Well, you wanted to do this alone, Shawn. Be a big boy and figure it out.

Upon reaching the gas station, he pulled his hood up over his face and shuffled inside. There were only a few other patrons, an elderly woman buying lottery tickets, a pair of teens messing around at the drink station, and one guy in a ball cap browsing the junk food.

Maybe I should get some supplies while I'm in here.

Shawn selected the biggest bottle of water they had in stock, a bag of jerky, and a couple of candy bars. Not exactly healthy, but enough to keep him energized in the short term. Caffeine might be good too, if he wanted to stay on the road for a while. He filled a large cup with coffee and headed to the register.

"Also want fuel on register three." He handed the clerk a fifty dollar bill. "Put whatever is left after the snacks on the pump."

"Will do."

As the clerk scanned his items, a prickling sensation crept across Shawn's neck. He turned around and saw the guy in the ball cap, a white dude of maybe thirty, eyeing him. The man looked away.

Shawn dipped his head. *Don't be paranoid. Get in, get out, don't look suspicious.*

The door chimed. Someone entering or exiting? He forced himself not to look. Situational awareness was one thing, but acting like a jumpy cat would only make things worse. He gathered up his items and headed out.

He stopped short. The man in the ball cap stood a little ways from his car, phone out. Was he photographing the license plate? Shawn took a step closer. The guy moved away, still holding his phone out in front of him, maybe just texting.

I need to get out of here, but I also need gas. If I hear sirens, I'll dump the car and fly out of here. I'm the only flying type sable in Ohio besides my dad and sister. Unless they've called in out of state support, they won't be able to catch me. I've got this.

Keeping a side eye on the guy with the ball cap, he placed his purchases in the car before starting to fill the tank.

The man put his phone in his pocket and wandered off. Shawn relaxed slightly. The pump dinged. He refastened the gas cap, slipped behind the steering wheel, and pulled out of the line. Almost immediately, headlights burned in his rearview mirror. Another car exited the parking lot right behind him. His pulse rate quickened, but he forced himself to stay calm. Probably a coincidence, but he'd take a roundabout route before getting on the interstate, just in case. He drove until the first light then took a right. The car followed. He accelerated a little above the speed limit only to find traffic slowing as they approached the next light.

As he drove, he went over the chances of the guy being another sable in his head. Near impossible for a hero. DOSA tended to keep track of those, and he knew everyone stationed in the area due to his father's position. Of course, villains were harder to monitor and there were the occasional outliers who managed to stay non-DOSA without necessarily being criminals. If the guy was a normie, then Shawn could handle him. Another sable, though, and he could be in for a fight.

He tapped his fingers anxiously against the wheel as he idled at the red light, trying not to glance constantly behind him to where the car still lingered.

Traffic started to move again. Shawn took a hard right at the next intersection, slipping into the turning lane at the last possible moment without using his signal. His tail followed suit. A horn blared.

Shawn sped up. There was another light ahead, this one yellow. If he could just squeeze through—

He gunned it, slipping through the intersection an instant after the light switched to red. The car halted behind him. His shoulders relaxed, but it wasn't over yet. He took another turn, then another. After several more, he had absolutely no idea where he was, but he hadn't seen any sign that he was still being followed. He pulled into the parking lot of a 24-Hour drug store and drew his phone out of his pocket.

"Okay, how far am I from the interstate now?" He brought up his map app and waited as it zeroed in on his location. He could see I-70 on the map, only a few miles away. He could be there in minutes. He memorized the route he needed to take and popped the phone back into his pocket.

The car shook, not dramatically, but as if he'd run over a bump even though he was parked. He froze.

Time to leave now! He threw the car into drive. A massive fist slammed through the windshield, aiming right at him.

Shawn yelped and summoned his powers. The fist bounded off his shield, the vibrations of the impact shivering through Shawn. Shawn pushed down on the gas, but a giant now loomed before him, tall as the neon sign advertising the nearby store.

Abounder!

The villain sidestepped the car, grabbed it from above as if it had been a toy, and shook it.

Shawn's teeth clattered together, every bone in his body jarring. Desperate to escape, he kicked open the driver's side door, unbuckled, and dropped. His powers activated a foot before he hit the ground. He spun into the air as Abounder flung the car at him. Shawn soared upward. The car flew beneath him, the wind of its passing stirring his hair. It crashed into the ground, rolling and crunching. Shawn shuddered.

Sorry, Jules. I guess you get my truck.

Abounder rushed him, his feet shaking the earth. A car alarm screamed.

Shawn dodged the villain's swinging fist.

I need to get out of here.

Abounder paused in the light of a streetlamp, sneering at Shawn. "Where's your pretty little girlfriend? The rumors I heard said she was with you, but when my cohort sighted you, she wasn't there. Tramp decide to cut ties when things got hairy?"

Rage stung the edges of the fresh wound in Shawn's soul. His teeth clenched. Maybe he could take care of one problem tonight instead of running from it.

Shawn whipped forward, shooting off three power blasts right in Abounder's face. The villain growled and covered his eyes with his arms. Shawn zoomed behind him, drew as much energy as he could into his fists, and dove into the back of Abounder's head.

The villain crashed forward. His hands skidded across the parking lot, leaving ruts several feet wide. Shawn rocketed up then let himself fall straight down. He crashed into Abounder's upper back—feet first. Abounder slammed into the parking lot. Shawn leaped up, ready to repeat the action.

Abounder shrank, his body retracting into itself like plastic wrap exposed to flame until he disappeared. Shawn landed in a crouch. His skin prickled. Abounder could be anywhere, ready to expand and strike—or he could be running.

He's not getting away again. Not after all this has cost me.

His fingers buzzed with pent up energy. Shawn pressed his hand against the pavement beneath him and channeled everything into a blast. The concrete cracked and rippled like water, waves of power expanding outward in ever growing concentric circles.

Abounder burst from the ground. He grew quickly,

flailing his arms to catch himself, but not quickly enough. Barely over the size of an average dude, he slammed into a nearby parked car. He stared up at Shawn, hazy-eyed, his mouth slightly agape. Shawn pulled the disruptor out of his pocket and rushed to whip it around Abounder's chest and arms. The villain grunted and writhed.

Shawn glared down at him. "I never did it. Maestro wasn't my kill. I had nothing to do with the robbery."

Abounder blinked at him.

"Not that it matters now. No one believes me, but at least I can give DOSA one last present." He pulled out his phone and sent a location tag to his father. He then clicked the photo option on the app. "Say cheese." He snapped a photo and shot it to his dad before typing out, **How fast can you get DOSA back up to me? I don't want to leave him alone, but I can't risk being here when they arrive. Not yet.**

It only took a few seconds for Dad to reply. **My team can be there in ten minutes. Good work, Shawn.**

Shawn hesitated. Abounder could have allies nearby who would free him if Shawn left. He paced around for a few minutes then flew to hover just out of the range of the streetlights. Obscured by darkness, he watched and waited, trying not to shiver in the cold winter air. The wind snaked around him, rustling his hair. Excitement over, his skin cooled.

"Come on, DOSA," he mumbled. "I need to get somewhere warm."

Finally a black SUV pulled into the parking lot. Shawn flew a little further away but still close enough to verify that the people emerging from the SUV took Abounder into custody instead of releasing him. When they started to set up police tape and create a perimeter, he decided he could leave.

He flew for a while, staying well above the city lights. He summoned a shield in front of him to ward off the cold air, and the expended energy got his blood flowing again. By the time he landed in a diner parking lot, he was cold, but no longer shivering.

I need to warm up, though, and also figure out what I'm going to do next. No car. No supplies. Cash is getting low. How much longer can I keep doing this?

Chapter Sixteen

Shawn took shelter in a booth at the back of the small diner, ordered a coffee, and sat holding the hot mug until his fingers started to thaw. He glanced at the wall clock. Almost midnight now. If DOSA were going to track him down, they probably would've by now. He needed to decide what to do. His plan had been to sleep in his car, but that was a wash. He could linger in the diner for most of the night, but he couldn't very well sleep there, and it was too cold to camp outside.

Do I have enough money for another hotel room? How do I even find a cash based hotel? Man, Katie was right. I'm lousy at this stuff.

Memory of Katie sent a pang of longing through his gut, and he closed his eyes. Part of him didn't even care if he got caught now. With Abounder in custody, it wasn't as dangerous anymore. Maybe a holding cell would be better than life on the run. At least his family would be able to visit him there. At least he'd have a bed to sleep in.

His head nodded towards his chest.

"You all right, sweetie?"

He jerked to attention. A portly waitress stood over him, steaming pot of coffee in hand.

"Yeah, sorry, just tired." He put his half empty cup on the table and allowed her to fill it.

"Maybe you should get home. You look like you could use some rest."

He tried to think of an answer but couldn't overcome the sensation of his last hope slipping away. Instead he shrugged.

She nodded knowingly. "If you need a place, there's a mission down on Grant that probably has a bed. No one should be alone this time of year."

"Yeah, I know, but I'll be all right." He let out a breath. "Just had a string of bad luck is all."

She smiled at him before slipping away. She returned a moment later with a slice of apple pie on a plate. "On the house."

"Thanks." This time he managed a smile.

He picked at the dessert. At least it gave him an excuse to stay in the diner for a little longer.

The sweet but tart apples and the flakey crust awakened his appetite. He had finished the filling and was picking up the last bit of crust to take a bite when his phone chimed in his pocket.

He glanced at the notification. *Burnr app: new contact request.*

He glanced around the diner then clicked on it.

Shawn this is Pliestocene. Let me know when you get this.

He paused before typing out, **How did you find my account?**

Your dad showed a screenshot of the message where you reported Abounder's location. I think he wanted to prove you were still with the good guys, but he forgot to crop out your contact handle. Not that it matters. This app is notoriously untraceable, and I just want to talk.

Shawn chewed his bottom lip. Rick was still the most likely candidate for being the actual traitor. Shawn couldn't let his guard down. However, he also couldn't turn away any potential leads. **What about?**

I'm sorry I jumped on you being guilty so fast. The financials Crystal showed me looked bad, but when you turned in Abounder, I looked deeper into it. It has to be Rapidz. She was the only one close enough to Carl to arrange this.

Shawn hesitated before replying. **Great theory, but do you have proof?**

Not yet. Working on it. The thing is, I can only do so much without making myself look suspicious. I've noticed she's slipped away from the team a couple times since Maestro died. She might just be going to get coffee, but she's cagey about it. I can't risk following her to see what she's up to, but you might be able to.

Shawn thoughtfully rubbed his thumb up and down the side of his phone. **How do I know this isn't a trap? How do I know you aren't the traitor?**

Can't help you there, pal. I just know unless we find out who really did it, you're not coming home.

Shawn closed the app without replying. On one hand, if it was a trap, it was a vague one. He wasn't being called to a specific place or time, just to generally follow Rapidz. He could do so from a distance, maybe. On the other, he couldn't trust any of his team members right now.

I'm running out of options and time. Even if it's a risk, it's at least hope. I need something to do, something to try, or else I might as well simply disappear.

The waitress returned. "You want another refill?" She nodded towards his half-empty mug.

"No. Thank you." He pulled out some bills and set them on the table. "Will this cover it?"

"Yup. You want change?"

"Nah, keep it. Thanks for cheering me up." He gave her a smile.

"I hope your luck changes, sweetie." She glanced past him out the window. "Oh, look! It's snowing. Maybe we'll have a white Christmas after all."

He followed her gaze. Flakes drifted through the darkness, catching the light of the streetlamps. They sparkled briefly before falling to the earth. In spite of everything, his despair lessened at the beauty of it.

I wish Katie were here.

An image of her standing in the snow, crystalline

flakes landing in her vibrant red hair, stirred a longing within him again. He shook himself out of it and headed out the door. He paused to think, taking in the cold kiss of snow upon his face. What was he going to do now?

If the team is working with the group that brought in Abounder, they are probably still in the Columbus area. Most likely in that same building where they interrogated me. That's not far from here. Of course, last time I trusted Rick, it totally backfired.

Knowing that the Burnr app deleted messages after a short time, he pulled up the conversation with Rick again and screenshotted it. He was not going to leave another exchange with Rick undocumented.

He cast one last longing look at the warm interior of the diner before stepping into the shadows and pushing off into the sky.

***

Shawn crouched on the roof of the building across from the DOSA office. A pair of unmarked DOSA SUVs and Rick's bike were parked out front. Even though it was well after midnight, several windows in the building were alight and occasionally he saw the shadows of people moving within.

Pulling a late night. Abounder's capture probably caused a lot of paperwork. He laughed quietly to himself. That was one advantage of the villain side. No need to file reports and fill out forms.

Shawn rubbed his arms and stamped his feet against the cold, his breath fogging before him. His eyes burned. He couldn't stay up here much longer. He needed to find shelter, someplace warm where he could at least get an hour or two of sleep before he faced another day on the run. Maybe the waitress was right about homeless shelters being a good idea. He doubted DOSA would be looking for him there.

A light flashed on the side of the building. A door opening onto a lit interior maybe? Keeping low to the roof, he hovered to where he had a better view. Yep, a shadowy figure slunk down the narrow alley, heading away from Shawn. From the figure's size and movement, he suspected it was Rapidz, but he needed to get closer.

He hopped across the street and landed on the roof of HQ. The figure picked up pace, going from a light jog to an easy sprint then to a blurring speed faster than any normie could match.

Yep. Rapidz. What is she doing out here at this time of night?

Still keeping as low as he dared, Shawn skimmed after her. She turned a corner, going deeper into a maze of small side streets. Definitely suspicious. Rick was right. She was up to something.

After about five minutes, Rapidz skidded to a halt at a deadend. Shawn froze, dropped down to street level, and peered around the corner where she now stood.

What is she up to?

He leaned out a little further. Something roared behind him, and he spun about, jumping into the air. A blast of ice hit the wall a foot from his head, shattering into a thousand shards. He threw up his shield. The pieces bounced off of him like driving rain off an umbrella.

Trap!

Rapidz rushed down the alley, straight towards him. He leaped into the air.

Another growl and a woman in a jetpack shot out of a side street heading for him.

He zoomed off, dodging bolts of ice. Rapidz ran along beneath him, easily keeping pace. Shawn pushed himself higher, looping over buildings Rapidz would have to go around. Crystal, who he now recognized as the one with the jetpack, sped after him. She wore a crash helmet with a visor that glinted in the city lights. Praying she hadn't had enough practice with it to keep up with his maneuvers, Shawn threw his power bursts in front of him, pushing himself into a backwards flip. He zipped past her in the opposite direction.

"Got eyes on him!" Rick shouted somewhere below. Shawn dipped several feet. A spear of ice swished over his head. A tower of the blasted stuff burst from the darkness of the nearest alleyway, Rick balancing on top of it.

Shawn dodged several more blasts before the roar of Crystal's jetpack sent his heart racing. He zipped out of there.

Ahead he could see a freeway overpass. If he could go under it low enough, she might not be able to match it. He surged forward. The hum of her thrusters grew louder by the second, and he already felt his energy flagging. Sometimes machine had some major advantages over man. Especially if that man was exhausted, cold, and on his last nerve.

He flew directly at the overpass as if planning to make a tight pass above it. Then, right when he reached it, he dove, shooting through the short tunnel like a blast of Rick's ice.

Crystal gave a muffled scream. Shawn emerged from the other side, hazarded a glance back, and stopped dead, hovering in place. Crystal lay in the center of the road, not moving. A semi barreled towards her. Its horn blared, but the sable team leader didn't flinch.

Oh, crap.

Shawn punched back with all his might, sending a blast of power behind him that shoved him forward at thrice his usual speed. He snatched up Crystal and skidded over the side of the overpass, crashing into the empty street below. Crystal moaned beside him, her visor cracked. She opened her eyes and stared at him.

I need to get out of here.

He staggered to his feet only to have a flash of silvery-blue rush up to him. Rapidz slammed a disruptor cuff across his chest and around his arms. He cried out as the irritating energy rushed through him, sapping his powers.

"Got him!" Rapidz crowed. She then glanced at Crystal, and her smile faded. "Boss, you okay?"

"Yeah, thanks to—" Crystal stopped, swallowed, and picked herself up, staring at Shawn.

Shawn staggered back a few steps. Weakness flooded his muscles. Even without the disruptor, he didn't think he had it in him to run any longer. If anything, he felt relieved.

It had ended. Maybe not the way he'd hoped, but his time on the run was over.

"Where's Rick?" Crystal asked.

"A few blocks away. He's a slowpoke," Rapidz said. "What do we do now that we've got him?"

"Take him in." Crystal rubbed her lower back. "I don't feel like walking, and I've had enough of flying for a long time. Can you run back to HQ and get the car?"

"Sure, boss." Rapidz cast Shawn a spite-filled glance. "You're finally going to pay for what you did to Maestro."

Shawn managed a half-hearted "I didn't—" before Rapidz blasted off at full tilt.

Crystal continued to consider him, her gaze piercing. "Why did you come back for me? You could've gotten away."

"You would've died if I hadn't," he said. "It was the right thing to do."

Headlights flashed across their faces. Crystal yanked him off the road to stand under a streetlight.

"Saving my life doesn't somehow cancel out what you've done."

"I swear I didn't do any of it," Shawn said. "I didn't take the diamond. I didn't kill Maestro."

"You say that, but you can't prove it, and now I catch you stalking, Rita. She told me she thought someone had been following her lately," Crystal practically spat the words. "I suspected it was you—"

"It wasn't! This is my first time!" Realizing what a

lame excuse that was, he calmed his tone. "Look, I only decided to follow her tonight because Rick messaged me saying he was suspicious of her and thought she might be the true traitor. I didn't know if I should believe him, but I was getting desperate."

Crystal narrowed her eyes at him. "Rick messaged you how?"

"Burnr app."

"The one that automatically deletes conversations?" She snorted. "Convenient."

"I took a screenshot." He twisted so that the pocket holding his phone was closer to her. "Please, look. Phone's in there."

She gingerly slipped her fingers into his coat pocket and pulled out the device. She thumbed through the few saved images. Her eyes widened, and she glanced in the direction Rapidz had left in. "You say Rick sent you this? Do you have any proof?"

"Only that he said it was him in the message, as you can see." Shawn's chest tightened. It hadn't even occurred to him that the person messaging him might not even be Rick. "Also, I still have his contact on the app. Sorry, that's the best I got. You can at least see that I didn't send the message to myself."

"Rick, get over here!" Crystal yelled.

With a zing and a swish, Rick slid in like a speedskater, skidding to a halt a few feet away. Shawn watched as Crystal hovered her thumb over the now open Burnr app.

"Do you have your phone on you?" she asked.

"Of course."

"Show me," she ordered.

Rick's brow furrowed, but he pulled the phone from an inner pocket on his biker jacket and turned the screen to face her. Crystal tapped the app, and his phone buzzed. A notification for a new Burnr message popped up on his screen.

He recoiled.

"So you suspect Rita of being the real traitor?" Crystal asked. "Why didn't you tell me?"

He avoided her eyes. "I wasn't sure who I could trust. I know you and her are friends. Figured with the kid having turned in Abounder, there was a chance we'd read him wrong."

"Huh. Okay. Sure." Crystal stuck Shawn's phone in her back pocket then skewered Rick with a hard-eyed stare. "Tell me how to spell your hero handle."

"What?" He took a step back.

"Pleistocene. You chose it because you've always been a paleontology geek, and every time someone in the press or on social media gets it wrong you whine about how it's not really that hard and how people should just learn to Google. So tell me. How do you spell it?" She crossed her arms over her chest.

Shawn's pulse raced. What was going on?

Rick gave an awkward laugh. "Crystal, you're being weird—"

"Spell it!" she snapped.

"Okay, sure." His stance relaxed, and he gave her an easy smile.

His hands shot forward coating Crystal in a sheath of ice. Shawn yelped and jumped back a step, but unbalanced by having his arms cuffed to his sides, he toppled, landing hard on his rear end. Inside her icy tomb, Crystal's eyes blinked.

Rick pulled a syringe out of his jacket. "You two couldn't leave well enough alone, could you?" He knelt and stuck the needle through Shawn's pant leg. Shawn fought the wave of dizziness for half a second then all went black.

Chapter Seventeen

Shawn's head swam, and his stomach churned. If he never took another knockout shot again, it would be too soon.

Don't do drugs, kids.

He pried one eye open. The room was dark, cool, but not outside in an Ohio winter levels of freezing. He could feel cold, dry concrete beneath his pants and a wall behind his back. Another person sat next to him, their body leaning slightly against his, their shoulders moving with in and out breaths.

He squirmed, but the disruptor still held his arms against his sides too tightly for him to move much. The person leaning against him gasped and jerked away.

"Who is that? Where am I?"

Crystal.

"It's me, Shawn," Shawn soothed. "As to the second question, I don't know, but I'm pretty sure Rick has something to do with it."

"He's not Rick," Crystal's tone tightened, as if she spoke through clenched teeth.

"You finally caught up, huh, Crystal?" A door opened allowing light to flood into the small, garage like space. Possibly the interior of a storage unit. Rick—or not Rick— stood near the door, arms crossed, a self-satisfied sneer on his face. "I guess the second half of your name isn't *Clear.*"

"What did you do to Rick, Maestro, you bastard?" Crystal snarled.

Cold washed through Shawn. "You mean ... oh crap. Is that even possible?"

"Apparently." The villain formerly known as Maestro ambled into the room. "It was a risk, but I'd backed myself in a corner. If I'd stayed in my own body, Abounder would've probably caught up with and killed me. It was a huge gamble, admittedly. I didn't know exactly what would happen to my consciousness if I jumped into another person right before my physical body died, but as you can see, it turned out all right." He stretched. "I'm a little disappointed though. I guess this isn't the worst." He waved at his body. "Powers are cool. Guy kept himself in decent shape, but he's like six years older than I was. What I really wanted was to jump into you, Park, but I can't puppet when a sable has his powers up like you did at the gas station, so I had to make a last second adjustment to the plan." He eyed Shawn. "Would've let me set the clock back a decade. Man, I'd kill to be in my twenties again—obviously because I tried to."

Shawn's skin crawled.

Maestro came closer, an evil smile pasted on Rick's face. "Also, I probably could've gotten a few nights with that hot redhead of yours out of it, huh? Man, what could've been."

Heat flared in Shawn's chest. He had never wanted to kill someone so much before.

"If you wanted to jump into his body, why did you frame him?" Crystal sputtered.

"That was a mix between a back up plan gone awry and happy accident." Maestro chuckled. "I knew if I took over his life, I'd want instant access to some cash, and also that my own belongings might be confiscated as evidence, so I hid some cash in his room and scheduled a bank transfer. I didn't anticipate you finding the cash, but I thankfully had time to reroute the bank transfer before everything got locked up tight for the investigation. I always knew I needed another option besides Park, though. That's why I called Rick to the meeting too."

"So, what, you just have Rick's body from now on and he's ... dead? Transported into your corpse?" Crystal pushed.

"Not sure." Maestro held up his hands. "Doesn't really matter. As long as I maintain control, he's not here." He turned towards the corner where some rubber totes and a few bags of what appeared to be concrete were stacked. "I had thought about swapping bodies after the first day, to further throw you guys off the scent, but apparently I can't access my own powers while in another sable's body, so I'm stuck with this one. Better than dead, I guess."

"There was never another traitor, was there?" Shawn frowned.

"Nope." Maestro opened one of the totes and removed what appeared to be a rusty hacksaw. Shawn stiffened as the villain examined it. Maestro shook his head and set it down again. "Too messy. If I'm really going to get away with this, I need to disappear you, Park, but it'll be better for me if they actually find Crystal's body. Make it look like you killed her. That'll keep them totally focused on you while I quietly slip back into Rick's life until I can find a buyer for the diamond."

"How did you even get it out of the bank?" Shawn asked.

"I puppeted the bank president when he was checking on the vault that evening. Got him to pocket it for me then let him go right when the vault closed behind him. He came to a little confused but people are all too willing to believe that they've just spaced out a minute or two. Much easier to process than that someone else was literally driving their body around without them." Maestro snickered. "He carried it out of the building without even knowing it then I grabbed him again and made him put it in a safe place. I haven't had a chance to go back for it yet, what with all the scrutiny on the team. Plus I wanted to make sure the blame was solidly placed on someone else before I risked having it in my possession, even temporarily." He picked up a screwdriver, turned it around in his hands a few times, then dropped it. "Going to go with the gun. Much simpler. Knew I shouldn't have left it in the glove box." He turned and winked at them. "Don't go anywhere, you two."

He exited.

Shawn strained against the disruptor, working his shoulders and holding his breath to try and get some space between himself and the metal bonds.

"I'm sorry, Surge," Crystal said. "If I hadn't been so willing to believe the worst of you, we might not have gotten to this point."

"Apologies later. Escape now." He wormed his way across the room to Maestro's tote of tools and kicked it until the contents spilled out on the floor. "Think we can use something here to get the disruptors off?"

"They're made of DOSA issued megasteel," she scoffed. "We're not going to get them off with a hammer and some WD-40."

"Worth a try."

A thought struck Shawn, and he wiggled over to the door, sitting just out of reach of the light. He listened. After a moment he heard faint footsteps approaching. He held his breath. He had one shot at this.

Maestro's silhouette filled the doorway. He took a step forward. Shawn kicked out. His legs tangled with Maestro's midstep. The other sable cried out, flailed, and toppled. He hit the ground. There was a metallic clank and something skittered across the floor—probably the gun.

Not ready to lose his advantage, Shawn rolled over and on top of Maestro, pushing him down with all his weight. Maestro clawed the floor, searching for his weapon.

"Check his pockets!" Crystal yelped. "He might have the disruptor remote."

Maestro's hand immediately darted towards his hip pocket. Shawn shifted his weight, falling to one side and

landing with his hip bone on top of Maestro's hand. He
ground down. Maestro shrieked.

With his arms still strapped to his body, Shawn could
only move from the wrists, but he managed to insert two
fingers into Maestro's pocket. He caught hold of
something hard and roughly the shape of a car key fob.

Maestro sent a blast of frost power downward,
pushing both men up. Shawn yelped as he lost his
balance and crashed off his opponent onto the floor. The
disruptor remote slipped from him. It slid over the floor
and out of reach.

"Enough!" Maestro hopped to his feet and punched
forward with both hands. Ice crashed across Shawn's
chest, pinning him to the floor.

Cursing under his breath, Maestro limped the other
side of the room and hit a light switch. "You're a pain in
the butt, you know that, Park?"

"That's what my sisters always tell me." Shawn
pushed against the ice. It strained and creaked but didn't
give.

Maestro scanned the floor, his eyes lighting up when
he sighted the handgun wedged in a corner. Shawn's
heart sank. He'd run out of time and out of moves. He
could only watch helplessly as Maestro crossed the room,
heading straight for the weapon. He cast a glance at
Crystal who sat, stony faced, awaiting her fate.

"What the—" Maestro screamed.

Something hissed. Shawn jerked his head around to
watch as the handgun morphed into a massive black
snake, surging upward, hood extended, red eyes glowing.
Maestro's face went white, and he stumbled back a step.

Hope flared within Shawn. He only knew one sable
whose powers could do that. A section of the floor rippled
ever so slightly. If Shawn hadn't known what to look for it
would've seemed a trick of the light. A camouflaged hand
reached the disruptor remote and pushed the button.

The disruptors fell from Shawn and Crystal, clattering

to the ground. Powers released, Shawn channeled his energy into shattering his frozen restraints. Shards of ice flew through the room as he jumped to his feet.

Maestro whirled around, jaw dropping. He shot two wild frost bolts, but Shawn dodged. Shawn fell to his knees, grabbed the disruptor, and pushed forward with one hand, sending a power blast right at Maestro's chest. The villain hit the wall with a sickening thud. Shawn sprang towards him, but Crystal moved faster.

His team leader grabbed Maestro by the collar as Katie flickered into her normal form beside Shawn.

Shawn let his muscles relax. "How the heck did you find me this time?"

She grimaced at him. "You kept the tracker, you idiot."

He slipped his hand into his pocket. Sure enough, the cold metal disk was still there.

"I was checking the DOSA emergency bulletins, and Rapidz reported her team missing after a run in with you," she continued. "Figured it was time to check the tracker again. So the bad guy was Rick?"

"It's complicated." Shawn frowned.

"No, it's pretty simple, really," Crystal growled, giving Maestro a shake. "You bodysnatched my best friend, Maestro. Tell me why I shouldn't murder you right now?"

He laughed. "You don't scare me, Crystal. You're all law and order and no gumption. Besides, I'm in that friend's body. You'd have to kill him to get at me." He gave the three DOSA heroes an irritating smirk. "What are you going to do about it? You should let me go. I might figure out a way to reactivate my old powers and transfer myself out of Rick eventually. It's the only chance the poor sucker has, after all."

A thought struck Shawn. He stepped forward, holding the disruptor cuff in front of him. "I mean, the only way you got into Rick *was* your powers which means the only thing keeping you in him probably is those powers."

Shawn fiddled with the disruptor. "What happens if you suddenly, I don't know, have those powers suppressed?"

Crystal's eyes widened. She snatched up her own recently abandoned disruptor cuff.

Maestro went rigid. "No, wait, don't!"

Crystal slapped the cuff across his chest.

Maestro convulsed. His head jerked back, and he let out an ungodly scream.

Katie flinched, grabbing onto Shawn's wrist. He slipped his arm about her waist and pulled her to him.

Maestro thrashed for a moment then lay still, breathing heavily. His eyes opened, and he gazed blearily up at Crystal.

"Where am I? What happened?" He tried to sit up but paused and stared down at the disruptor cuff. "Uh ... am I arrested for some reason?"

Crystal put her hand on his shoulder. "Tell me how to spell your hero handle."

"Uh, okay." He looked at her as if she was nuts but quickly rattled off, "P L E I S T O C E N E. It's not really that difficult. It's formed from the Greek words for 'most' and 'new' because it's geologically—"

She tackled him in a hug. "Oh, Rick, I'm so glad you're all right."

Rick gazed over her shoulder at Shawn. "Dude, you really need to help me out. What did I miss?"

"A lot." Shawn sighed. "Right now, though, I need to call my dad."

Chapter Eighteen

A short while later emergency vehicles of both the DOSA and normie varieties choked the small parking lot of the long term storage facility. Shawn's whole being lightened when his father pulled up and rushed to embrace him.

"I'm so glad you're safe." Dave held his son closer before releasing him. "And you too, Katie. I figured when you disappeared from the house it had something to do with Shawn."

Katie shrugged, walked past Shawn's dad, and settled into the backseat of his car without a word.

Shawn swallowed. She'd been standoffish since she'd rescued him, answering his questions about how she'd gotten there and if she were feeling okay with one word if not one syllable replies. Now, though—

"I think she's mad at you," Dave said in a stage whisper.

Shawn started.

"If you really think about it, I bet you can figure out why." Dave nodded towards the car. "Being a man is partially knowing when to apologize."

Shawn let out a long breath and walked to her. He stooped to gaze into the car. "Hey, you have every right to be upset with me—"

"Why would I be upset with you?" She stuck her nose in the air, refusing to look him in the eye. "It's not like you almost got yourself killed again for no good reason, probably taking stupid risks and making dumb choices like not checking your pockets for tracking devices."

"For what it's worth, I'm never giving you a hard time about tracking me again." He gave her what he hoped was a winning smile.

She sniffed at him as if he were a jug of milk slightly

past its expiration date.

Oh, boy.

"Okay, I'm truly sorry. I shouldn't have left you like that. It was cowardly."

"Why? Why should I care if you left me? It's not like we're an *us* or anything," she said, her tone cold but her eyes tearing up.

"Katie, babe." He knelt beside her. She turned her head away.

"It's not like I would've given up everything to help you stay safe, but you had to be a dumb big stupid hero and leave me alone where I had nothing to do but wait and pray that my boyfriend—or former boyfriend or whatever—didn't get himself killed. It wasn't like I spent the last several hours crying because I didn't know if I'd ever see you again. It isn't as if that matters because you're not my boyfriend anymore. You don't want to be —"

Stomach in knots, Shawn cast a helpless glance at his dad.

"Could you use an assist?" his father asked.

"Desperately," Shawn said.

Dave Park reached into his pocket and pulled out a small box. He tossed it to Shawn who caught it against his chest. Realization flooded through Shawn, and suppressing a grin, he turned back to Katie.

"You're right, Katie. I don't want to be your boyfriend anymore," he whispered.

She whirled to face him, lower lip quivering. "Wait! I'm not that mad!"

"Easy." He laughed before opening the box.

She inhaled sharply.

"I'm hoping for fiancé. Husband shortly after?" He leaned closer. "Does that sound like something you'd be up for?"

"I think you've earned that promotion," she whispered.

Happiness overwhelmed him. She slipped her arms around his neck and pulled him in for a kiss. Their lips caressed for a long, precious moment. His fingers found her hair, twining into it, savoring how soft it was, how real she felt. Finally he withdrew and carefully placed the ring on her finger.

"Perfect," he murmured.

She giggled. "Such a romantic proposal location too."

He followed her eyes and winced. "Dang it, I *am* the guy who proposed in a parking lot. Do you think I can have a do over?"

"Nuh-uh." She kissed his cheek. "I'm keeping this memory forever."

Crystal approached them. "I've got everything cleared with the investigatory agents for you to go home for the night. They wanted to keep you for interrogation, but I told them I could handle it. You've been through enough."

Weariness flooded Shawn. "Thank you."

"Look, Shawn, I really am sorry about everything I put you through. If you want to transfer off my team, I get it, but knowing what I know now—" She let out a long breath. "Young or not, inexperienced or not, I would easily put you in the top five of sables I've worked with. You're resilient, self-sacrificing, and resourceful when everything is against you. It would be my honor to continue working with you."

"I'll have to think about it. It's not personal, ma'am. It's just—" He stood and glanced from his father to Katie then back to Crystal. "I have things that are more important to me than DOSA, and while I'm always going to do my best at my job and for my teammates, my family is going to come first, always." He reached down and took Katie's hand. "I need to make choices that let me honor that."

"I understand." Crystal clapped him on the back. "Whatever you decide, I'll respect it." She walked off.

Shawn rocked slightly on his feet.

"You need to sit down?" his dad asked.

"I need to lie down and probably sleep for a week." Shawn yawned.

His father smiled. "I can facilitate that. Let's get you home."

***

Katie sat in the Park's living room, a warm mug of cocoa clutched between her hands and a blanket wrapped around her body. The Christmas tree lights twinkled and beyond that the snow fell. A fire crackled in the hearth.

Just like a TV Christmas. I thought I'd never get one of those.

Even her Christmas the year before with her mother hadn't been quite what she'd imagined. Her mom obviously loved her, but the time apart and the starting of a new family made Katie feel more like a guest than a family member. Somehow the Parks had managed to make her feel at home in just a few days. She raised her cup to her lips. As she did the diamond on her engagement ring sparkled in the firelight. Her heart danced within her.

This truly was a dream.

Ears ambled into the room and nosed at her knee. She put her mug on the coffee table so she could rub his ears without worrying about spilling. It was now afternoon. The rest of the Parks had gone out to do some last minute shopping. It had been almost two days since Shawn had returned home, and Christmas was tomorrow. Shawn and Katie had decided to stay in to get some alone time.

"You look cozy." She looked up as Shawn entered the room, a warm smile on his beloved face.

"I am." She patted the couch next to her. "It's good to be still again." He settled beside her, and she rested her head against his shoulder. "I called my mom and told her about our engagement. She's happy for me."

156

He arched an eyebrow. "Did you tell her about everything else that happened this week?"

"No, I didn't want to worry her. Thankfully she intentionally doesn't watch the news over the holidays. Says it ruins the mood."

"That's good. Oh, speaking of news, Crystal texted me. They retraced the bank president's route after the diamond went missing and found it. In a gym locker, of all places. Guy didn't even know he'd hidden it. Poor sucker."

"At least that's over." She nestled into him.

"Yeah." He squeezed her knee before clearing his throat. "I've been talking to my dad. He wants to try and pull some strings to get me reassigned to his team."

Her smile broadened. "That would be amazing."

"Yeah, it would. I've always wanted to work with him, but I was worried that it would look like nepotism if I started my career directly under my dad, so I didn't pursue it." He wrinkled his nose. "Everything that happened has kind of cured me of that reluctance."

"I bet."

"I've also been talking to him about you," Shawn continued. "Dad thinks that if Rain is willing, we might be able to get you moved to Columbus with us. I mean—I know you like your team, but I like having you with me too, and I have to think if you—"

"I'd love that!" she said quickly.

"Good." Shawn kissed her, first on the forehead, then each cheek in turn, before settling on her lips.

She sighed contentedly. "Oh, Shawn, could things be more perfect?"

"Well, my sister could forgive me for getting her car wrecked and relinquish her claim to my truck." He grimaced.

She giggled. "I am not going to put money on that happening."

"Dad says the insurance might pay out, considering it

was technically a criminal act that totaled her car. If so, she might get a check worth enough to mostly satisfy her. I am going to see if I can save up enough to put some money towards her car fund. It wasn't fair what happened."

"Maybe not, but I think she understands," Katie said. "She's a superhero too, after all. She knows how dangerous it can be."

"Less dangerous with the right people at your side." He held her hands between his, his gaze so intense that she couldn't return it. "If the mess with Maestro taught me anything, it's that I can't do this on my own. I need the people around me. My team and my dad, yeah, but most of all you, Katie. You're my most important person, and I'm not ever going to be stupid enough to let you go again."

"You better not." Her laugh came out in an awkward, mousy squeak.

His eyes warmed. "Man, I love your laugh."

"Good, because it looks like you're stuck with it." She leaned forward to kiss him again, her heart full and every dream about to come true.

The End

ABOUT H. L. Burke

Born in a small town in north central Oregon, H. L. Burke spent most of her childhood around trees and farm animals and always accompanied by a book. Growing up with epic heroes from Middle Earth and Narnia keeping her company, she also became an incurable romantic.

An addictive personality, she jumped from one fandom to another, being at times completely obsessed with various books, movies, or television series (Lord of the Rings, Star Wars, and Star Trek all took their turns), but she has grown to be what she considers a well-rounded connoisseur of geek culture.

Married to her high school crush who is now a US Marine, she has moved multiple times in her adult life but believes home is wherever her husband, two daughters, and pets are.

For information about H. L. Burke's latest novels, to sign up for the author's monthly newsletter, or to contact the writer, go to
www.hlburkeauthor.com

and sign up for the author's newsletter!

Free eBook for Newsletter Subscribers!

Also by H. L. Burke

For Middle Grade Readers
Thaddeus Whiskers and the Dragon
Cora and the Nurse Dragon
Spider Spell

For Young Adult Readers
An Ordinary Knight
Beggar Magic
Coiled
Spice Bringer
The Heart of the Curiosity
Ashen

The Nyssa Glass Steampunk Series:
Nyssa Glass and the Caper Crisis
Nyssa Glass and the House of Mirrors
Nyssa Glass and the Juliet Dilemma
Nyssa Glass and the Cutpurse Kid
Nyssa Glass's Clockwork Christmas
Nyssa Glass and the Electric Heart

The Elemental Realms Series
Book One: Lands of Ash
Book Two: Call of the Waters

The Dragon and the Scholar Saga (1-4)
A Fantasy Romance Series
Dragon's Curse
Dragon's Debt
Dragon's Rival
Dragon's Bride

The Green Princess: A Fantasy Romance Trilogy
Book One: Flower
Book Two: Fallow

Book Three: Flourish

Ice and Fate Duology
Daughter of Sun, Bride of Ice
Prince of Stars, Son of Fate

To Court a Queen

Spellsmith and Carver Series
Spellsmith & Carver: Magicians' Rivalry
Spellsmith & Carver: Magicians' Trial
Spellsmith & Carver: Magicians' Reckoning

Fellowship of Fantasy Anthologies
Fantastic Creatures
Hall of Heroes
Mythical Doorways
Tales of Ever After
Paws, Claws, and Magic Tales

Match Cats: Three Tails of Love

Supervillain Rehabilitation Project
Relapsed (a short story prequel)
Reformed
Redeemed
Reborn
Refined

Blind Date with a Supervillain
On the Run with a Supervillain

Made in the USA
Middletown, DE
26 June 2022

67813527R00099